Also by Elizabe

Jock McLock's Piratic:

The Gryphon Key

Bethloria Series:

Firelight of Heaven

Greenheart of the Forest

Her Non-Fiction Books:

Comedy Theatre for Upper Primary

Teacher Resource Book

Comedy Theatre for Upper Primary

Student Book

Doorway to Adventure

By

Elizabeth Klein

Copyright © 2019 Elizabeth Klein

ISBN: 9781705726815

Junior Fiction: A collection of short stories. Fun and adventure, animals, spooky tales, bullies, fairy tale retelling, aliens, inventions that go wrong, myths and legends.

Ages 8 – 12 years

Contents

Dragon Tale

Summary: *It's bad enough when Amelia's parents are eaten by a bad-tempered dragon, but when her strange aunt arrives to take care of her, Amelia believes the woman may be downright dangerous. Or is she just trying to help? And why does she think Amelia is an alien?*

Amelia Lockhart knew that her parents had been gobbled up by an ill-tempered dragon living in the woods behind her house. But no one in the whole wide world believed her. Teachers at her school said the dragon was simply a figment of her imagination since Amelia was very good at inventing stories. The sympathetic police officer stopped writing in his notepad when she mentioned the word *dragon*. Her archery instructor said Amelia often pretended to hunt dragons and other mythological creatures, so her story could well be made up. Neighbours believed Amelia's parents had disappeared on purpose because she was a feisty, unruly tomboy. That tore Amelia up more than anything and she didn't speak to the few neighbours who came to the 'funeral', or in fact, to any of them ever again.

That evening, Aunt Izzy, who lived in a purple caravan and roamed around the countryside like a vagabond, drove up the gravel driveway and parked beside the house. She had come to look after Amelia in her parents' rambling old house.

'So sorry, Amelia dear, for not being able to get to the funeral,' she said, peering over the top of her tortoise-shell glasses. 'I was just ... too far away when I heard the terrible news. But I'm here now.'

Amelia didn't know her aunt very well, but decided early on that she was indeed loopy, probably because she had lived alone with her pet goanna, Charlie, for many years. But Aunt Izzy was the only person who truly believed that her parents *had* been eaten by the dragon. Maybe she believed Amelia because she idolized large lizards. And well, dragons were a particularly large variety of lizard!

'Tell me again, dear, what you think happened to your dear mother and father,' she asked Amelia next morning.

Dressed in floral pyjamas, she sat sipping tea from Amelia's mother's favourite teacup while swinging her crossed leg back and forth. Amelia's butter knife paused in the air as she looked across the table at her. How many times did she want to hear how they disappeared? She had

5

already recounted the unfortunate events twice already. Amelia took a deep breath and placed the knife beside her toast.

'A week after we moved here, Mum was cleaning the attic when she found some old papers stuffed in the wall.'

'In the wall, you say? How fascinating! Go on dear.'

Aunt Izzy took another sip of her tea, her eyes never leaving her niece's. One of her hands rested on Charlie's head. The goanna, draped across her lap like a beaded blanket, was also watching Amelia. It was strange how reptilian her aunt's eyes looked in the dim morning light that streamed in the kitchen window. Amelia looked at the nearby woods, aware that her aunt was staring at her, waiting for her to continue. She cleared her throat.

'The papers looked very old. One of them said there was a dragon living in the woods and whoever lived in this house had to be careful.'

'Simply thrilling! And you showed these papers to the police, didn't you?' Aunt Izzy asked, peering over the top of her glasses, appearing almost jubilant.

Amelia sighed and nodded. 'But they just thought it was some kind of prank.'

'You believed the papers though, didn't you dear?'

'Yes.' Suddenly Amelia found herself reliving the painful events of that fateful morning. 'Mum and Dad went for a stroll before breakfast, which is what they always did back in the city. They wanted to explore the woods. Mum said it looked mysterious and beautiful. They left me asleep in bed except I wasn't asleep. I looked out the window and saw them going into the woods. They were holding hands.' Her cheeks heated. She never meant to share that. Swallowing the lump in her throat, she went on. 'When they hadn't returned by lunch time, I realised something was wrong. I didn't know what to do.'

'You poor thing,' Aunt Izzy crooned, her hand wrapped around the teacup. 'Whatever could someone as young as you do in such a terrible situation?'

Amelia didn't need to be reminded of how young she was. At twelve, the authorities said she was far too young to live on her own. If it hadn't been for Aunt Izzy coming to look after her, Amelia knew she would have been placed in an orphanage. That would have rubbed salt on her already wounded heart. She had a lot to thank her aunt for, although living with Charlie was a little awkward and unsettling. For one thing, Amelia had to watch where she placed her feet when she walked about the house, or else trip over the lazy reptile.

The goanna was long, much longer than a cat or a dog and its wrinkly skin looked loose, as if it was much too big for its body. It had bands of yellow running across its neck down to the tip of its powerful, snake-like tail. Every few seconds a pale, forked tongue would shoot out of its alligator-shaped mouth, which Amelia found disgusting.

'I called our neighbour, Mrs Warren,' she said, 'who came over with her husband. We waited till tea time but still Mum and Dad didn't come back. That was when Mrs Warren called the police. They came and searched the woods but found no trace of them. They brought in sniffer dogs but for some reason they wouldn't go in among the trees so they took them away. The search went on through the night, but ...'

Amelia choked back tears. Images of an enraged dragon devouring her parents still made her weep into her pillow late at night. Having to retell it was all too much.

'That's enough dear,' her aunt said softly and patted her arm. 'No need to say any more. I know what happened.'

Her aunt poured another cup of tea from the teapot. Staring at the trees outside, Amelia struggled with her emotions. Then something wet and fleshy touched Amelia's bare arm. Startled, she turned to look at the goanna as it flicked its forked tongue towards her again. *Ughh!* She slid her chair away from the table, out of its reach.

'What'll we do, Aunt Izzy?' she asked.

'We plod on dear, as if Frank and Doris were still alive.'

'What about the dragon? It's still there in the woods.'

'Ah yes, the dragon,' Aunt Izzy's eyes gleamed. 'I'm going to tell you something now that will sound outrageous, even unbelievable. But I need you to focus, Amelia, on what I'm telling you.'

Charlie winked at her. Amelia was beginning to feel uneasy. She didn't want to hear anything *strange*. Having a resident dragon living in the woods behind her house was strange enough. Groaning inwardly, she gave her aunt a nod.

'It's very important that we Lockharts stick together. After all, there are no more of us anywhere ... in this universe.'

'What do you mean *in this universe*?' Amelia asked, not really wanting to know.

'Before you were born, your parents and I came from somewhere ... very far away to settle here. And I'm not talking about an overseas country either! I'm talking about somewhere further than that!'

As her aunt talked, Amelia decided that she wasn't loopy at all. She was a dangerous psychopath! Underneath the table, Amelia gripped the tablecloth with tight fists. What was she going to do? Her parents were dead and her aunt was a lunatic! Was an orphanage such a bad place after all?

9

Her aunt went on. 'In fact, the three of us time-travelled from our home-planet Tangowene, all the way to earth.' She gave a little giggle.

Amelia gasped. This was worse than she imagined! Now they were aliens!

Oblivious to her niece's reaction, her aunt continued. 'We were forced to leave our dear planet because of an alien invasion by the Nagas, a particularly nasty, reptilian species wanting to breed in our lovely pink oceans. We Tangowenes had to ...'

Amelia squirmed in her chair as her aunt's voice droned on. Finally, she raised her hand and her aunt stopped speaking. She blinked at Amelia. Charlie's forked tongue shot out in rapid succession.

'None of that is true, is it?' Amelia snapped. 'You just made it up because everyone said I made up the dragon.'

Hot tears pricked at the back of her eyes and she shook as hot rage overcame her. How could she be so stupid, thinking her aunt—or in fact anyone—would believe her? It would be better off living in an orphanage where she wouldn't have to tell anyone how her parents had died. The terrible secret would remain hers forever and she would never share it with another human being again.

'I knew you wouldn't understand or believe me,' her aunt said, 'so I brought along our bodyguard. Meet Charlie, the Nagas hunter. Beware, he's not what he seems.'

Amelia was about to leave the room in outrage when Charlie slipped off Aunt Izzy's lap and began to squirm on the kitchen floor. Its body flipped back and forth and its legs flailed about wildly as if it was in terrible pain. Horrified, Amelia stared at the reptile, thinking it was probably sick, soon realising it was, in fact, changing shape.

'Don't be alarmed dear!' her aunt called as Amelia stumbled back in alarm and collided with the sideboard.

Larger and larger the reptile grew until its enormous head nudged the ceiling of the kitchen, whereupon it stopped growing. Its monstrous body was squashed against the four walls and hid Aunt Izzy from Amelia's sight as she stood frozen, not daring to move in case the monster decided to swallowed her.

Just then, her aunt's head popped out from behind one of the reptile's hind legs. She grinned and pushed her glasses up the bridge of her nose.

'Well, dear,' she said in a breathless voice. 'Now do you believe me?'

All Amelia could do was nod her head. Her aunt patted Charlie. 'That's enough now.'

At the sound of her voice, the reptile began to shrink again until it was once more the size of a goanna. Amelia didn't move a muscle, though her legs wobbled underneath her like a bowl of jelly. She reached for her chair and slid onto it, staring at Charlie and her aunt.

For the next three hours, Amelia asked many questions about Tangowene and the Nagas. She listened in awe as her aunt described their beautiful home planet far away. Then Aunt Izzy admitted that she had placed the old papers inside the attic warning Amelia's mother and father that one of the Nagas was in the woods hunting them.

'You put the papers there?' Amelia stared open-mouthed at her aunt. 'But how? They were ancient.'

'Remember I said we *time-travelled*? Well, that's what I did. Almost a hundred years ago I came here and placed them in the attic for your mother to find. And now that you *do* believe me,' her aunt winked at her, 'perhaps we should work together on a plan to rid the Nagas from the woods before it gobbles us up too. After all, you come from a class of warriors on Tangowene.'

Amelia was surprised how thrilling that suddenly sounded to her. It explained why everyone thought she was so feisty and unmanageable. It also explained why she loved adventure and horse riding and archery. They were all part of the nature of a warrior.

She sat forward in her chair and stroked Charlie's head as she listened to her aunt. The creature's forked tongue flicked out and Amelia thought she saw a smile on its broad mouth. It didn't seem disgusting any more to her. Nor was her aunt loopy or a dangerous psychopath. She had to admit that life with her aunt would prove challenging and exhilarating at the same time. But Amelia was really looking forward to going dragon hunting with her Aunt Izzy and Charlie, the Nagas hunter.

'After all, my dear,' her aunt said, 'hunting Nagas was what you were born to do.'

Zac's Terrible Idea

Summary: *Some kids have a knack of having terrible ideas, as Rem discovered when he went to meet his friend, Zac. Making a kite on a very windy day happened to be one of them. But what happens when the kite plucks Zac off the ground and into the air? Find out by reading the story.*

"Hey Rem!" called Zac. "Meet me outside the Robinson's this arvo. I've got an idea."

Rem groaned as he watched his best friend wave to him from the bus window as it sped off. Zac was always inventing things. Rem was always the one getting hurt. He was certain that Zac's idea had something to do with that pile of junk outside the Robinson's house. It was Clean-Up Week and people had been placing their rubbish outside for the Council to pick up all week. One man's rubbish was Zac's treasure.

Rem walked home and dumped his bag in his bedroom.

"I need you to go to the corner store," his mother called from the kitchen.

"All right," he said, "but I have to be quick; I'm meeting Zac."

His mother poked her head around his bedroom door, frowning. She seemed to know about Zac's *ideas* even before Rem did.

"Make sure you keep out of trouble. And don't come home bruised!"

She gave him some money to buy bread and milk. He ran all the way to the corner store and all the way home again. Was Zac already waiting for him at the Robinson's house? They did have the best pile of junk in the street. Rem was certain Zac's idea had something to do with it.

The last time Clean-Up Week was on, Zac had built a go-cart out of old bits of wood, rope and pram wheels. He had found them among the Robinson's pile of rubbish. Rem had been the official tester of the go-cart. Zac had taken notes on how fast it went. Everything had gone smoothly until two yappy dogs appeared from nowhere and began chasing Rem down the hill. Terrified, he had forgotten to steer the go-cart. It went like a rocket and even flew like one too, right into the ditch at the end of the road. He was off school for a whole week with a sprained ankle. That hadn't been such a bad thing, except his mother had not been very happy with him—*or Zac!*

"Don't be late for dinner," his mother called as he raced down the footpath.

"Okay!"

A strong wind had picked up by the time he reached the Robinson's. Zac was on top of a pile of old furniture, rummaging through it. He waved to Rem and climbed down with a ball of string in his hand.

"Over here!" he called. A huge, home-made kite was lying on the ground. A couple of old drawers sat on its wings so it wouldn't take off while Zac looked for other things he needed. He held up his hand and grinned. "Look at all this string. It's just what I was looking for."

"A storm's coming, Zac. You won't be able to hold onto a kite in all this wind," Rem said.

"Sure I will. Just hold it while I tie the string on," Zac said and began to wind the string tightly around the kite's middle while Rem held onto it. "There. Now it's finished. Help me get it up."

When Rem picked up the kite, the wind whipped it out of his hands. It lifted the kite into the sky. Zac held onto the ball of string, but the wind was too strong. It began to lift him off the ground, too. Before he could think, Rem jumped and grabbed his legs.

"Let go!" yelled Rem, but Zac was too scared. His eyes were like huge saucers as he stared ahead.

Up went the kite. Up went Zac and Rem. A small black and white dog appeared from nowhere and chased them down the street. It barked and growled. Before Rem

16

could lift his feet out of the dog's reach, it latched onto his right shoe. Rem yelled and shook his foot until the dog let go and fell into a bush. Somehow, Zac's inventions always attracted dogs! They seemed to go nuts.

Rem held tightly onto his friend as the wind lifted them higher. Soon his fingers began to slip. He lost his hold and slid down Zac's legs, taking his friend's shorts with him. Only his red underpants stayed up. Rem shook his head while Zac laughed!

Then the wind took them over a low fence. It tore Rem's shorts and scratched his legs. He yelped and clung tighter onto Zac. They drifted across the road, right in front of a car. Rem and Zac yelled! The man and woman in the car yelled! A small dog in the woman's arms yapped and bared its teeth at them. Rem closed his eyes, expecting to get splattered all over the window. A sudden gust of wind lifted them up just in time. Rem opened his eyes and let out a long sigh.

They drifted over a field. Tree branches whipped Rem's chest and face. A small mob of kangaroos stampeded when they saw them coming. Rem and Zac sailed right over the paddock, past the gumtrees and toward the houses.

"You know, this isn't such a bad way to see the countryside," Zac said after a while.

"That's easy for you to say!" Rem growled. "You're not bitten and scratched raw."

Zac just grinned and stared ahead. The wind blew his hair around his calm face. He was enjoying the ride. Rem's arms felt stretched in their sockets and he was certain they were twice as long. He didn't think he could hold on much longer. All of a sudden, a huge tree loomed in front of them.

They were heading straight for it!

"You have to let go or we'll be killed!" Rem screamed.

Zac let go of the string. They both landed with a loud splash in someone's pool. Two fox terriers appeared from nowhere and started barking at them. Zac and Rem took off in a mad dash for the fence. Zac was trying to run and pull up his shorts at the same time.

The dogs nipped at Rem's heels as he dragged himself over the fence. They were on a riverbank. He leaned against the fence, dripping wet, scratched and bruised. He was certain he would have to limp all the way home and *then* be killed by his mother. Zac just grinned as he stared at the river.

"That was so much fun," he said.

Then his eyes widened as a branch came bumping along in the fast current. "Hey Rem, I've just had another great idea."

Alteration

Summary: _Braeg's alteration into a sneal is a complete success. Everything is going well. Then the ship crashes. Or has it? His worst nightmare is realised when space pirates board the ship and discover him in his altered state._

The feel of the air was changing, not in degrees, but in texture. Light dwindled. Mirrored sky lamps blurred. Sounds faded. The last thing Braeg heard was Caiwyn's voice.

'You'll be all right.'

She sounded hollow, as if caught inside a tunnel far away. She faded. Everything disappeared.

Awareness came, but no actual thoughts filtered through his head. They had ceased. He was aware of shifting and being shifted. A dissonant sound reverberated through his eardrums, convulsing his body. Muted rumblings sounded far away, yet near. He did not possess emotions and he did not recognise time, here, just existence. Lights flickered in his eyes. Eons passed. Braeg reached out and touched something soft like thistledown. He could feel textures and move about.

Pain. He flinched. Scarlet flowed around him; now he was aware of discomfort, intense and sharp, a cutting pain. He writhed, opened his mouth, gurgling in the fluid, then closed it again. He never had such alteration as this before and a sense of trepidation washed over him, and exhilaration. His hands reached up and something firm clamped over his wrists and held them down.

Pressure! He couldn't move! He felt sharp, excruciating pressure along his arms and legs, then more scarlet fluid swam past his eyes. A loud shriek of fear pounded through his veins. It was coming from him. He struggled and kicked.

The feel of the fluid around him was changing, not in degrees, but in texture. A firmness. The pain receded to a distant thought. He tried to move his limbs but the fluid had grown sluggish, like congealed pudding. Everything slowed down. An age passed and the stars wheeled overhead.

Fragments of memory returned. He was lifted, laid upon layers of soft furs. His neck felt too weak and wobbly for him to turn his head. Light shone dimly from one of the sky lamps so it wouldn't hurt his eyes. He opened them in thin slits, then all the way and blinked several times. Blurred shadows passed. He lifted the new limbs where his arms had once been. He could flap them now. Yes, he saw shiny black flippers. A new body, remade for a watery existence. For a time.

Something came close to his face and he felt fear again. The thing made a sound and two blue orbs opened and closed. In a corner of his memory, he recalled that it was a human face. *Caiwyn?* That name was familiar. The face smiled and her long appendages tugged at something on his neck.

'You're almost finished now,' she said.

He understood her words. Yes, that's what those sounds were.

'You look great. Sky Wind will be impressed.'

Impressed? By what? Braeg opened his mouth to ask her. A strange sound gurgled from his own lips. Lips? Glancing down, he noticed a black snout with long, wiry whiskers. He looked up at Caiwyn.

Please don't forget I'm human! Please!

She smiled again. 'We won't. You'll need the water, as soon as I adjust your gills. But not yet. Not until you're strong enough. How do you feel?'

Scared, he admitted. *Wish I could talk to you.*

'That's understandable,' she said and ran her warm fingers down his left flipper. Her touch felt so odd and his flesh tingled. 'Now rest. I'll be back soon to release your gills. Promise.'

He lay on his stomach and gazed at the small lights in the walls of the cabin. When he closed his eyes, he saw fish darting in the ocean. Small, silver fish, the sort he loved—*to eat?!*

Danger! It lurked in the seaweed forest that grew from the murky, ocean floor.

Don't go there! His friends warned. *Something dark and frightening lives in there.*

He could see its monstrous shadow coming closer and closer—

His eyes snapped open. He had been dreaming, but something *had* woken him. A jolt. Where was Caiwyn? The hologram clock on the wall showed that several hours had slipped away since he had last seen her. But what was time when you were a—*sneal?* He'd laugh, if he could. His family would—

He slid off the table and crashed against the wall.

Hey, what's happening? Where's Caiwyn?

The walls shuddered and pieces of ceiling and debris showered him. Then he knew that the thing he was in—a sky ship—must have crashed into something in space. But what?

What ... is ... happening?

He stared up at a shiny panel of bright lights. He shuffled along the floor towards the door. The controls were too high for him to reach to open it. He tried to stand, but as a sneal he couldn't.

A scream echoed inside his tiny eardrums. It came from outside, in the corridor. Something was wrong. He lurched away from the door.

Please, don't let it be space pirates! Not now! Not when I'm … like this!

Just then, the door slid open and Braeg glanced up as two men strode into the lab, holding light guns. This had to be his worst nightmare. Waist-length dreadlocks and looped earrings dangling from noses told Braeg they were space pirates. They stopped when they saw him and smiled.

Nooooooo! Please, I'm human! Caiwyn! Help me! The loud squeals came from his snout.

'Well, what have we here?' one of the pirates said and licked his broad lips. 'Captain will be happy with this find.'

The other raised his light gun and aimed.

No. Please, I'm human! You're making a terrible mis—

Hidden

Summary: *This fractured fairy tale is as timeless as the forest and hills. Yet it is not told through the eyes of the expected main character, but from one who is more cunning. Misunderstood, he lurks behind the trees, watching … and waiting. He's good at that.*

I watch her pick wildflowers at the edge of the forest. She likes the same purple trumpets and milky-faced ones that my mother likes. I smell them dying in her arms. One by one, she places the long stalks carefully in a homemade wicker basket at her feet. Sunlight bathes her young face in a wash of gold. Even at this distance, her eyes remind me of tiny snatches of the blue sky through the forest canopy, her skin white as cream. Everything about her moves me. I stand motionless beside the silver-grey birch and stare at her through the dappled shadows.

When the basket is full, she picks it up and carries it in the crook of her arm back along the forest trail that people sometimes use. A spray of sunlight showers the forest floor around her hurrying feet. Doesn't she know how dangerous this forest is with wolves prowling about?

And lately, I've spotted an occasional bear with its cub foraging for roots and berries. The warm weather has coaxed the large predators out of their winter dens and they're hungry after their long slumber. Sometimes the mournful howls echo through the forest as packs of wolves hunt along the old trails. They won't hesitate to attack a young, defenceless girl out on her own.

Is she tempting Fate being out here, or what?

I start to notice things about her. The scarlet gown clipped at her throat with the silver brooch glows like a fiery sunset. In this forest, everything else is a shade of green. Don't get me wrong, I prefer green. It spins subliminal messages through the shadows where I like to wander, where I practise being hidden, as I'm doing now.

The girl doesn't hear me following her as she looks about the towering trees around her, wide eyes filled with wonder. I've lived in harmony beneath this tangled roof all my life with my mother and father, and I'm familiar with everything that occurs here. All its sights, smells and sounds. It's a beautiful forest. I feel the rhythm of its seasons flow through my veins, the warmth in the air that heralds new beginnings, new life, new visitors. Of course, that's when the forest is loveliest. Yet sometimes I wonder about the wilder lands my mother speaks of, where the earth pushes itself up and stands tall, where the tips are snow-drenched and frosty. Where there's little or no sunlight.

The skies are different there, my mother once told me, *bluer somehow.*

Yeah? One day I may see those distant lands for myself.

But right now?

The girl takes the trail to where the charcoal burners live. It's not a pleasant place. What's out there? Carcasses of trees, stripped of their green hides by the woodsmen, my father told me, and their rough wood huts that reek of smoke. Slabs of wood snaked together with vine rope, stained tin roofs and conical piles of dead wood. And stinking, smouldering piles of charcoal.

Fire, the terrible sting...

Yes, I know. I know to keep away; my father often likes to warn me.

But this girl isn't like them. Dying wood stench doesn't cling to her. She's akin to the stars I sometimes see through the branches, the lonely stars, a spectacular being who has stepped down among mortals. A far beauty beyond my reach. Of course, I'm over-exaggerating, like my father.

The girl knocks on a door and it swings open, safe in the smell of newly baked bread. I take a deep breath as an old voice gathers the girl inside the hut. I practice hiddenness behind the birch as I wait. And watch.

How many people live here in this charcoal burning community? Six? Eight? And now the girl.

A tawny-haired man appears carrying steel and wood. He uses it to split stumps apart and then stack them in that great heap on the charred earth. The man is huge like a bear, another sort of hunter I must watch out for. But he doesn't notice the shadowed observer at the edge of the clearing.

Not until one of the scrappy hunting dogs lifts itself onto its haunches and starts to bark do I steal away, back into the forest, back into the shadows where I'm safe. Maybe one day, when I don't feel so shy and timid, I'll say hello. Until then ...

I wander away. Thoughts of home and my family fill my head. My father likes to hunt through the corridors of towering trees for our food. He knows the ancient trails better than anyone, even better than the charcoal burners. Yes, he knows how to blend into the shadows. But I am not like my father.

Face your fears. Don't flee them, he sometimes tells me. *Come hunt with me.*

All right, I will! Promise! You don't have a clue that I'm afraid of the fever, the terrible fury inside you that might one day surface in me.

My mother likes the marshy valleys and meadows. I don't fear her. She likes to wander through the ragged drifts of white mist that rises from the damp forest floor.

It's the best time to see deer and elk ...

My mother tells me this whenever its misty through the trees, hoping that I'll start to hunt with my father. But I love the beauty of the forest too much to take of its life. Deer, bear, marmot, squirrels, wolves, even the charcoal burners live in harmony here, their voices creating a concert of existence too fragile to destroy.

A movement ghosts through the trees and I hold my breath. A black, shaggy wolf glides between the trunks as silent as a shadow. It's a huge male, dragging one of its back legs. But it hasn't spotted me, nor has it picked up my scent. *Careful!* Down to the stream it slinks, over the moist, mossy roots that stretch like old, stiff limbs. And there, in the fading half-light of evening, thirsty deer seek respite. The wolf, I can tell, is a master of hiddenness and none of them see him approach.

Until it's too late.

Until it charges straight for the youngest, the fawn, furiously snapping at its tender throat. The rest of the deer flee and fear ravages my heart. The fawn's life-force fades and scarlet mingles with the flow of water at its struggling feet. Its grief soon ends. The wolf carries the fawn up from the stream and home to its hungry family. I watch the scarlet water vanish, and I'm haunted by the fawn's grief as it struggled in the great jaws of the wolf.

Long before dawn breaks, I race to the edge of the forest, to the meadow where I first saw the girl. Maybe the warm air will entice her out of the old woman's hut and draw her here. The sunlit meadow is full of drifting pollen and the song of humming bees. Small birds flit among the grass, disturbing the insects. I doze among the cool, damp trees, but I never really sleep. The forest is an exciting yet dangerous place and I don't want to be surprised by one of its many hunters.

After many sunsets, I see a wash of scarlet stirring among the moss-covered trunks. My breath catches in my throat. It's the girl! Straight into the meadow she wanders, carrying the wicker basket in her hand. At last she's come to pick more wildflowers.

I'm captivated by everything about her. At her long, glossy black hair that reminds me of a dark night without stars. Her beautiful scarlet gown with its deep, satin-lined hood. Her face, so childlike and—

I leap to my feet!

There, at the edge of the forest, among the shadowy trees, crouches the huge black wolf that drags its hind leg. Its crazed red eyes glow like live coals, focussed on the unsuspecting girl. My heart thumps painfully against my ribcage, then it races so fast it hurts. Fear grips my throat and squeezes until I can't breathe.

No no no no no! Please not her!

A red haze of memories fills my mind. Of the suffering fawn and its violent death. Of the rabid wolf that kills anything that moves. Yes, I've often seen and feared it. The cruel hunter now becomes my adversary. I must distract it somehow so the girl can run away like the deer. If only I could call out and warn her, but I can't speak her language.

I lift my muzzle and howl.

My father sees me and snaps the empty air savagely. He'll deal with me later, I know. For now, his eyes revert back to the girl, crouching in the long grass. I smell her fear as she screams. I bound toward my father but the tawny-haired man reaches him first and throws a well-aimed block of wood into his side. With a shrill yelp of pain, my father struggles to find his feet. The woodsman runs straight at him with the steel and wood he uses to cut stumps apart. Heightened terror courses through my father's feverish blood as he springs for the man's throat.

The man leaps aside and swings the steel at my father's head. I hear the dull thud and watch as the great black wolf falls to the ground.

The man jerks the steel out of my father's mane and glances about the trees but he doesn't notice me. I step back into the shadows. My skin shudders, but not from the cold. I watch the man comfort the crying girl and lift her onto her feet. He picks up her basket and together they walk back to the charcoal burners' community.

In the deep silence, the rhythms of the forest sink into my being like a heartbeat. And I realise that one of the pivotal lights in my life has gone out, like a bright star that dashes across the universe only to be swallowed by the blackness.

I step into the meadow, now cold and grey. My fur shudders. The sentient part of me wants to see my father for the last time; another part of me dreads what I'll find. I sit in the grass and remember the look on their faces as they walked past him.

On light toes, I walk toward the black wolf lying dead in the grass. I sniff the carcass. I smell the fever inside him, still hot in his fur. What shall I do? Leave him for the other predators to consume? I know that is the natural way of the forest. Sadness pricks at the back of my eyes. But I mustn't remain here in case the tawny-haired woodsman returns.

Madness takes hold of me, a madness that comes from cruelty or hunger, or perhaps both. With one last piercing howl, I turn away from the black wolf. My father. I run through the unforgiving forest without pausing for breath, far from the charcoal burners' community. And the girl in scarlet. Vengeance, black and violent, stirs inside as timeless as the stars, as cruel as the grave. A new heartbeat. And a new appetite, yearning to be fed ...

Once, the girl in scarlet had captivated me with her beauty. In my heart, she was like an exotic flower whose seed had drifted in from a pleasant dream and taken root in the meadow soil, nourished by the rain and sun. But I don't see her in the same way anymore.

Pain and trauma push out my fascination with the girl. Amongst the beauty of the forest, there's ugliness, coarse as freshly butchered life. In time, I'll forget the black wolf. His presence will fade from my thoughts, but this eager blackness within, so patient and cold, will endure. I know where the fire stench lives. I know to avoid the tawny-haired woodsman. But I also know where the old woman lives. I'll enjoy eating her when the time is right. And I'll especially enjoy the tender flesh of the girl in scarlet.

The thought makes me howl with ravenous delight.

Fall of the King

Summary: *King Arthur is dead and Bedevere, one of his most loyal knights, feels the terrible grief of a future without him. As he and Merlin set the King upon the funeral raft, it is gathered by the mists of Avalon.*

A sword plunges between a gap in the armour and the King drops to his knees.

Around me, the lake shudders and darkness descends. A thorn of grief impales my heart. That impending chill enfolds me, for I know the prophets do not lie. On this fateful day the throne shall pass to the Queen. Even now, she paces the lonely corridors of her cold castle as she waits for her lord to return.

I, Nymue, Lady of the Lake, sense Emrys breaking free of my binding spell and slipping from my cavern stronghold. Magic weaves after him but each thread tears asunder beneath his renewed power. Hurrying to the battlefield, he arrives too late, for the hammer stroke has fallen and the echoes of war already fade from the Plains of Camlann.

Somewhere on the plain, a knight regains consciousness. He does not know how long he has lain among his lifeless comrades. The iron taste of blood fills his mouth. He pushes himself up into a sitting position, bends over and spits it out. It leaves his mouth dry. Burdened by his heavy armour, he rolls over and clambers onto his knees, and then to his feet. Gritting his teeth, he draws a measured breath and sways. Blood trickles down his shirt. He reaches up and feels his side with the tips of his fingers. His flesh burns.

Hunching against the pain, he drags his broken blade behind him as he stumbles forward. The stench of smoke wafts through the air. In careful scrutiny, he moves among the fallen and his eyes scour the Plain. Hour upon hour, the knight staggers through the carnage until, at last, he hurries to the side of the one he seeks. Breath catches in his throat.

The King's blue eyes flicker and open. 'Bedevere?' he mutters.

'Here, my lord.'

The King licks his dry, bloodied lips. 'Where is my sword? Where is Excalibur?'

Bedevere casts his gaze about the field of broken swords and burnt shields. Breathing through his teeth, he struggles to rise, his armour heavy, and spies the great sword lying near the slain body of Mordred, King Arthur's foe. Retrieving it, he stumbles back to the King, whose eyes are closed as if in slumber. For a moment, an anxious moment fills the knight's heart.

'My lord,' he calls in a desperate voice. The blue eyes flicker. 'I have your sword.'

'Bear me to the Lake,' the King says.

Confused, Bedevere stares at him. 'The lake, my lord?'

'Where the Lady and I first met. There I shall tryst with her one last time.'

The words bring a hard knot of sorrow to Bedevere's throat. Slowly, he struggles to raise the King onto his feet and, with one arm about his waist and the King's arm about his shoulder, he bears him from the battlefield. Past the endless fallen, the knight staggers on with the King.

His mind begins to wander, caught in a strange dream, bathed in the red haze of exhaustion and of a curious disorder, as if he were a character in a tragic tale and none of this was real. Groaning, he pushes himself on. Each jerky step sends a fresh jolt through his body. He has not gone more than three bends in the road when he cannot put another foot in front of the other. Every part of him hurts. Pain gnaws at his side.

I must stop.

At the edge of the road he collapses with the King and dreams, time spinning away until cold shadows fall across them. The sound of heavy wheels intrudes upon the cloud of silence. *Am I imagining ghosts?*

'Is it you, Emrys?' the knight mutters.

Through the murk, he sees the cloaked wizard crouch beside the King. Then Emrys lifts them both onto a wagon and they continue their silent journey.

The road runs beside sodden fields where turfed ramparts plunge like amber spears into distant forests where the wild boar roam. The feverish knight becomes aware of the honeyed evening light as the sun slips closer to a jagged, dark horizon. His memories keep the journey in focus as the shadows of his fallen companions—friends who were once precious to him—parade before his vision, their ethereal voices rising and falling like chittering larks among the flowering gorse. Lancelot... Gawain... Percival... all who once sat at the round table in Camelot. Dead, fallen at Camlann.

Bedevere listens to the sloughing breath of the King. Tears blur his vision. *He is leaving us.* The knight strokes the King's ashen face and the eyelids flutter. In a frozen moment, Bedevere waits, but the blue eyes do not open. The knight drifts into the rhythm of the trundling wagon and slumbers while the lonely night watch falls to Emrys.

At daybreak, a broad stream appears, glistening in the sunlight with tall rushes on the far bank and silver willows straggling the running water. Before them the diamond-studded glints of a great lake appear and fast-flowing channels that meander through the valley. Down to the shores the wagon rumbles. Upon white, smooth sands it comes to a halt.

Heart grieving, Bedevere assists Emrys with the King, still clutching the great sword in his clammy fist. Together they bear him to the water's edge where King Arthur collapses, dribbling blood from his pale lips. Grey and weak, he opens his eyes to behold the lake.

With a ragged sigh, he calls, 'Bedevere... take my sword, Excalibur... Toss it into the waters.'

Confused, the knight glances up at the wizard and receives a gentle nod. 'Do as he says.'

The darkness of war rolls back and I rise from the cold lakebed, ready to take back my gift and welcome home the King to Avalon.

The knight struggles to his feet, still grasping the magical blade, now as heavy as a tree. Carrying it, he staggers to the shore where he sways, staring at the vast, misty waters. And then, the knight lifts high the sword and swings it twice above his head before releasing it. Over the lake it spins. Once, twice...

I reach up and seize the hilt, holding it steady in the chill air before drawing it below the dark, swirling waters. Down into the bowels of the lake I swim with Excalibur.

'Come! He is dead!' calls Emrys. His voice cracks like a broken note.

As the knight turns, he notices a raft fashioned with freshly cut wood, lashed together with vine to form King Arthur's funeral bier. He hadn't noticed it before. Was it there all along? Bedevere chokes back a ragged breath and fear of the future squeezes his heart till it hurts.

The King is dead!

So much pain and death in the world! Dizzy, he staggers toward Emrys and together, they place King Arthur gently upon the bier. That one, terrible thought screams anew through his mind.

The King is dead.

The knight watches Emrys push the raft out into the lake, but he does not light it. In silence, they stand and watch the whirling mist gather the raft with its sleeping King.

The knight weeps.

Camelot is bereft of its King. Dark days of war will follow and courage and hope will fail. King Arthur had led them into the light with Merlin's aid, had defeated many strong foes. They will now gather like storm crows on the horizon and who will they look to for aid? The wizard? The Queen, an inexperienced woman?

Grief clutches at his throat. A firm hand settles upon his sagging shoulder. He looks up into the wizard's gaunt face.

'You must return, Bedevere,' says Merlin. 'Tell the Queen what has befallen her King. And tell her—'

He does not finish. He turns instead to the wagon and begins to unhitch the horse.

'Will you not return with me?' asks the knight, confused.

'No.'

The wizard assists him onto the back of the horse. Bedevere clutches the reins with a rasping sigh. He nods at Merlin. The knight slumps forward on his mount, then begins the long, slow journey back to Camelot.

Forgotten Stars

Summary: _Small children often imagine friends to play with, but what happens when that friend is a ghost? Will is left at a deserted house by his mother and imagines not just his playmate, but her mother too._

At the end of a dusty road stood an emu looking at the deserted house. Around the rust-stained roof, piles of leaves and twigs had accumulated in its gutters, and long drifts of dry eucalypt leaves had strayed across the porch and lay piled up against the wall. Through a cracked window, filthy green curtains stirred in the breeze. The movement startled the emu and it strolled off down the road.

Inside the house, a boy craned his neck and stared at the emu's graceful walk until it wandered out of sight. It was hot inside the house and the boy, whose name was Will, could feel his t-shirt sticking to his back. Before she'd left, his mother had warned him the temperature might climb and had left him a bottle of iced water and several cans of soft drink in a bag along with a dozen bars of chocolate. These had mostly melted in their wrappers.

Despite having eaten two of the chocolate bars, Will's stomach still rumbled. He took no notice, however, since hunger was not new to him; loneliness and impatience were. But it was pointless to feel impatient. His mother was doing everything she could to find them a new home. He'd wanted to help, go with her, but no matter how much he'd cried, she hadn't allowed it.

'You can't come with me this time, Will,' she had said. 'We can't be seen together. You'll be safer here. Promise.'

Using the worn sponge from her compact, she'd dabbed the bruise under her left eye and moved it gingerly across the cut on her bottom lip. She then patted the residue powder across her pinched cheeks and forced a smile.

Sullen and angry, Will had slumped against a bare wall. He'd raised his knees, hid his face in his arms and cried, hoping she'd change her mind and take him with her. But when he looked up, she had gone. He had raced to the door and looked outside, only to see the raised dust from her blue Fiesta. He raced down the veranda steps, clutching the soft, filthy wool of Mr Peabody in his grubby hand and had shouted into the wind for her to come back while tears streaked down his cheeks. Cicadas had drowned out his voice but he shouted until his voice sounded croaky and hoarse.

The first hour in the house after his mother left had been the worst. To distract himself from sad thoughts, he'd wandered through each room, looked at the crumbling paint on the walls and the broken fixtures. He'd counted seven rooms in all, each thick with dust and decay. The floorboards creaked as he walked barefoot over them.

We'll stay here a while, his mother had said. *No one will look for us here. But if someone comes, not a peep! Understand?*

He watched dust motes glitter in the afternoon light that streamed in through the broken blinds. Will waved his hand through them, sending them somersaulting through the air. For a long time, he sat and stared at them, and began to imagine things.

He noticed shadows moving about the house. He hadn't seen the narrow bed before, with its pink eiderdown and the frilly pillow cover on the single pillow. A doll, dressed in olden-day clothes, sat up against it with cloth-sewn arms and legs. Its blue, doll eyes stared ahead on its cloth face. Another single bed with a blue eiderdown and a blue pillow case nudged the opposite wall.

A girl laughed and he spun around. The sound prickled his skin. The bed faded into the afternoon shadows as the sun dipped below the tree-line. The dust motes stopped swirling. Will stepped back, anxious to leave the room.

Hurrying outside, he noticed how low the sun was, glittering through the gums. Already, mulberry hues spread across the sky and more cars were speeding home on the highway below, like scurrying beetles.

Will sat on the top step on the porch and listened to them. Maybe if he concentrated on his mother, she'd return and take him away. Maybe he wouldn't have to spend the night on his own in the strange, abandoned house. Whose was it anyway? His mother hadn't told him when she drove up the dirt road to the front steps.

What if its owners returned and found him there on his own? What would they do? The police might be called and they would take him away. Then he'd never see his mother again.

Stay hidden, understand? Rob won't find you here. No one will.

Rob was his father. Something had happened between him and his mother so they couldn't live together any more. Something bad. His father had exploded yesterday and had broken some of their furniture. He'd even punched a hole through one of their walls in his rage. Angela, his mother, had cried as she grabbed Will's arm and dragged him to her Fiesta. She had driven so far that Will had fallen asleep, finally waking at the house with his mother slumped over the wheel, crying afresh.

Why is Dad so angry? He'd asked.

She'd looked up at him with red, swollen eyes. Because he likes his beer more than us.

Will's eyes clouded with tears. He didn't want to think about his father like that, not loving him and his mother any more. The yelling and smashing of crockery he was used to. He'd learned to zone out, but...

The floorboards creaked behind him. He spun around to look, his heart racing. Normally, strange noises didn't bother him, like the peach tree branch that scraped across his bedroom window in the wind. Or the sound of the next-door neighbour's irritating Jack Russel barking at everything that went on in their street. Or Mr Piper's rooster that crowed at all hours of the night and day. Or his parents fighting.

A hot wind stirred the eucalyptus-scented air and jangled the leaves on the gums. Screened by a patchwork of bushes, the cars on the highway below flashed past in streaks of colour and sound. They never stopped. Horns blared, sirens wailed, brakes squealed, hot engines whined, beasts of steel that never slumbered.

People commuted along that road to the city where he and his mother had lived in a rented apartment until yesterday. They had lived on the sixth floor with dozens of strangers they almost never saw except in the elevator on the way to school or to the shops. From their lounge-room, their view had been a red brick building five metres away. Sometimes he could hear every word coming from the window opposite, in which case, their neighbours must have heard all the fights coming from their apartment. But yesterday, everything had changed when Will's father arrived home drunk from the pub.

Moisture prickled Will's eyes as he sat on the cracked veranda and stared with longing at the empty driveway, willing his mother's car to reappear, to climb the hill back up to the house where he waited. Will imagined his mother jumping from the driver's seat, running towards him and wrapping her arms about his small frame, smothering his cheeks with kisses.

Clutching Mr Peabody to his chest, Will scrubbed his sleeve across his wet eyes. His aching heart sank to his shoes when he realised he might have to face a night on his own. With a sobbing breath, he turned and stared at the house. At the vacant windows that stared back at him and the open door that gaped in sympathy. Emptiness stretched inside him as vast as the sky above. No matter how unbearable her departure had been, now he simply accepted that he had to wait here for his mother until she returned.

Will stood up and went inside and closed the door, then he went to look for his backpack. Inside the flap, he noticed he had six Mars bars and four coke cans left. The trouble with opening one of the cans was that the sweetness attracted bugs. The last one he'd left half-drunk so he could return later to finish it off but was now crawling with small black ants.

Clutching a soft Mars bar in one hand and Mr Peabody in the other, he walked around the house to the back veranda and pulled the broken screen door back. The wooden door was rotten at the bottom, where leaves and dust had blown into the room beyond. He pushed it in and stopped to look at the room that had once been a kitchen. Dusty light streamed in through the filthy windows. Will noticed the black iron stove, grimy from disuse, green-painted shelves, some still with a few blue plates and cups sitting on them. There was a dark sideboard against the wall, its small, glass windows cracked, its curved legs ending in shapely curved paws.

A family had once lived here. He could hear the echo of their laughter through the house. Or glimpse the shadow of a woman who wandered about. He saw a little girl reading a story out loud from a book. Will huddled on the floor against the wall and listened to her voice.

Sometime later, his head lolled forward and he jerked upright. He must have fallen asleep. Where was he? What time was it? He had no sense of time because he didn't own a watch. But the shadows on the grimy floor seemed longer and he was aware of the patchy sound of cicadas in the eucalypts outside, not the continuous thrum that had earlier hurt his ears. And his stomach grumbled again.

Feeling lonely, Will wandered outside. He walked about the yard, staring uninterested at the overgrown garden. A leaning clothesline stood on a cracked square of concrete. In the corner of the yard a wire chicken pen stood overgrown with grass. Will paused to look inside. The tiny concrete floor was muddy and strewn with rotting leaves. Hens once pecked in here, he thought, and had roosted in the broken boxes at the back.

A clump of wild irises grew outside the pen, near the wire, deep purple folds with flecks of lemon. He reached down to stroke one of the flowers. It felt soft and velvety between his small fingers.

He could see the woman and the girl moving about the yard as they collected eggs, hung the washing on the clothesline or crouched beside the garden. He trailed behind them, blinking as each scene faded in and out. They couldn't see or hear him. So, were they real? He didn't know.

As Will began to walk to the front of the house—coming from the opposite direction this time—he suddenly noticed an old stone well. Green moss slurred the stonework and gangly weeds nestled all around it. Will waded through the long grass and peered into it, but it was dark and he couldn't see any water. A broken wooden bucket lay behind the well and the hand-pump was rusty.

'Hello!' Will called and was answered by a faint echo.

He called again, this time a little louder. The echo, too, sounded louder. Then he picked up a stone and dropped it into the well. *Thud!* It sounded empty, so Will continued around to the front of the house. He sat down on the filthy top step beside his bag and faced the road again.

That's when he'd noticed the inquisitive emu poking about in the yard. He'd never seen one that close before, so he ducked inside the house. At first, he feared it might enter through the broken door and peck him with its sharp beak, but his fears were soon allayed when the bird strolled down the road without a second glance at him.

The shadows grew cold and the din made by the cicadas had diminished. Their sound reminded him of the long, droning songs made by the stars. That's what his grandmother used to tell him when they lived in New Zealand. She'd cradle him in her arms when he was small and rock him back and forth to the sound of singing cicadas.

It's just the stars singing, Will, she'd say as she stroked his hair.

Her home was a sugar-and-spice kind of place. A place that made you feel warm and cosy on the inside. Afterward, he'd drift off to sleep and ride an enchanted ship in the sea of heaven. All night, he'd sail the stellar waves near the singing stars until morning light found him tucked up in bed, his head filled with dreamy songs. How he'd loved those stories. But his grandmother was a whole world away in New Zealand and couldn't help him or his mother here.

He wandered into the part of the house that had once been a living room and sat down on the rug. Frowning, he ran his fingers over the plush pile and wondered why he hadn't seen it before. Then he blinked at several wooden trunks standing about the floor, the lid of one open and partially filled with crockery.

Mesmerised, he watched as the woman suddenly walked into the room, humming to herself. She was carrying an armful of folded linen which she deposited into the trunk before closing its lid.

Will started. *Where did she come from?*

He didn't dare move lest she notice him and call the police. He was, after all, trespassing. But the woman seemed oblivious to his presence and came and went several times more, packing another trunk with folded clothes. Will watched her in silence for a long time, until his eyes glazed over with boredom.

Then the girl—no older than he was and wearing an olden-day dress with white stockings and a pair of big-buckled shoes—skipped through the door carrying the rag doll he'd seen on the bed. His eyes brightened and he sat up. She stopped when she noticed him and a smile formed on her pink, rose-bud lips.

'Hello,' she said as she approached. 'What's your name?'

He hesitated. 'Will.'

'Would you like to play with me?' the girl asked.

The girl's mother wandered into the room again, arms laden with plates. 'Who are you talking to, Riana?'

'My friend Will,' she replied and pointed to him.

'I've told you not to make up stories, Riana!' the woman said with an angry frown. 'Now go outside and play while I finish packing. Dinner will soon be ready.'

'Yes, mamma,' the girl said and gestured to Will to follow her.

He trailed behind as she led him outside. The sun had already set but she didn't seem to mind the coming darkness.

'Would you like to pat my pony?' she asked.

Pony? Will frowned. He hadn't seen any animals in the yard apart from that wandering emu. 'Where is it?'

'Why, it's over there!' She pointed to the corner of the yard and there, with its head down grazing, stood a small, white pony. Will started. Why hadn't he seen it before? They hurried over to it and the pony raised its head to look at them.

'You can pat him if you like,' Riana said. 'Like this.'

She began to stroke the pony's neck and yellow mane. Will, feeling a little frightened, hesitated before he walked up to the pony and patted its neck. The girl smiled at him.

'I'm Riana. What are you doing here anyway?'

The question caught him off guard and he didn't know what to say. The girl, seeing his reaction, shrugged.

'It's all right,' she said. 'You can sleep in the other bed in my room. It used to belong to my brother, but he went to live in heaven.'

Will knew she meant her brother had died. He wasn't sure he wanted to sleep in someone else's bed, especially someone who'd died. He didn't say anything.

'My brother's name was George and he was sick all the time,' Riana said. 'You're a quiet boy, aren't you?'

He nodded. Just then, Riana's mother called from the back door. Riana giggled and clasped his hand in hers. It felt soft and warm.

'Come and have dinner with us. Mother's cooked some rabbits.'

Will's face twisted. He'd never eaten a rabbit before, but his stomach rumbled so loudly he allowed the girl to lead him inside. What would her mother say? She couldn't even see him. But as he neared the back door, he noticed the woman smiling—*at him!*

'Who's your friend, Riana?' she asked.

'His name is Will. Can he stay for dinner? Please!' Riana pleaded.

'But won't his mother have dinner for him at home?'

'I can stay for dinner,' Will said.

The smell of roasting rabbit wafted out into the back yard, reminding him just how hungry he was. The woman shrugged and gave a friendly nod.

'You can stay and have a little then. Just make sure to wash your hands before you come inside,' she said.

'All right mother,' Riana said.

Dropping Will's hand, she began to skip around the side of the house. Will hurried after her and halted at the well, which looked as if it had been cleaned up and recently used. He blinked. That's not possible! He noticed the hand-pump wasn't rusty anymore and the bucket was attached to a rope.

But it was all broken! he thought. *And there was long grass everywhere!* Yet now it was mowed, neat and tidy around the well!

Riana began to pump the hand-pump. Soon water sloshed out the sluice and they washed their hands.

'Come on Will,' she said. 'I'm hungry!'

Me too! he thought, trailing behind her to the back door. Riana's mother appeared, wiping her hands on a white, frilly apron tied about her waist.

'Will, I'm glad you could join us for dinner,' she said and stepped aside for them to pass. In the small dining room, she pointed to a wooden chair at the table. 'You can sit beside Riana if you like.'

Riana giggled as he sat beside her and his face became hot. The table was set with a floral tablecloth, silver cutlery and glass tumblers. Will had never seen a table set so well. Riana's mother brought in a large casserole dish full of rabbit stew and then a platter of roast potatoes and orange pumpkins. Last of all, she set a small pan of steaming peas on the table and the gravy. It looked like a feast to Will. The stew smelled delicious and his stomach rumbled loudly.

After saying a quick prayer over the meal, Riana's mother heaped their plates with a generous dollop of the stew, some vegetables and then poured the thick gravy over it all.

'Well, don't just stare at it!' she said with a good-hearted chuckle. 'Eat up before it grows cold!'

And that's just what they did. Will didn't stop eating until his plate was almost empty. Then Riana's mother—whose name was Isabelle—jumped up from her chair.

'Goodness me! I forgot something!' she said and hurried into the kitchen, returning a moment later with a basket of home-made bread—except she called it damper. Will mopped the gravy up with a thick slice of it and then sat back in his chair, feeling contented and full.

'How was that, Will?' Isabelle asked, slopping up her own gravy with a slice of damper.

'That was the best meal I've ever had,' he replied truthfully. His mother wasn't a great cook and he was used to eating lots of take-a-ways.

Isabelle looked at him sympathetically as she ate her damper. 'Where is your mother and father?'

The question made Will feel very uncomfortable. But before he could answer, the sound of a car pulling up outside sent Will jumping from his chair, startling Riana. It had to be his mother, returning to take him away at last.

'That's Mum now!' he said with much excitement and could barely contain himself. 'I have to go! Thank you for dinner!'

He raced through the deserted rooms of the house and flung the front door wide just as his mother climbed out of the car. She held a white plastic bag. Will ran straight into her outstretched arms, tears streaming down his cheeks. But he wasn't crying because he was sad anymore; they were tears of joy. His mother kissed his forehead and they hugged for a long time.

'Oh Will,' she said, 'I'm so sorry I left you here. I never meant to stay away this long. I brought some fish and chips for tea. You must be starving!'

'Mum, I'm full!' he exclaimed. 'I had dinner with my friend Riana and her mother. Come and meet them.'

'Sweetheart, there's no one here,' his mother said, looking at him concerned.

'Yes there is!'

Will took his mother's hand and led her through the house, determined she should meet them. He stopped when he saw how dark it was inside. He called Riana's name. The empty house echoed back.

'But I ate with her and her mother!' he said, looking confused. 'She had a pink bed and a white pony. I patted him.'

His mother wrapped her arms about him. 'Let's get out of here. I got some plane tickets so we can go live with grandma. Would you like that?'

Will was still looking around at the dilapidated room when his mother's words sank in. He squealed with delight and they walked outside, holding hands. As his mother drove away, Will glanced back at the dark house one last time and thought he saw the shadow of a little girl standing on the porch, waving goodbye.

An Easter Proposition

Summary: *A school can be a scary place for adults, as Sam soon discovers. He notices 'things' that children take for granted. But the figure at the end of the corridor is the scariest. Why is Sam there at all?*

As Sam pushed aside the tall, wrought iron gates, their rusty hinges screamed in his ears. His legs froze. A shiver raced down his spine as hundreds of curious eyes turned in his direction, their owners fleetingly paused from their boisterous activities. It was as if the heartbeat of the world had stopped, allowing him just a moment to enter another world where a slate-grey sea of giggles and stares met him. Then, as he took his first step, the world's heart began beating once more and those frenetic activities resumed. He took a deep breath.

Just get it over with, he told himself.

Sam trudged toward the red brick building. It looked so imposing in the sunlight, so bleak and uninviting. He plodded up the short flight of stairs to the twin open doors, thrust wide like the mouth of a monstrous creature. He noticed how chipped and flaky its blue paint looked. *Needs another coat*, he thought impulsively.

Then Sam peered down the endless, dark corridor deprived of light. *Maybe there's a blackout.* At the end of the corridor, he could make out a closed door. It seemed to beckon in a macabre sort of way. He shivered.

Come on, you know why you're here, he berated himself. Licking dry lips, his legs started moving again. *Yeah, I know.*

Halfway along, panic seized him afresh. The high-ceilinged corridor seemed cavernous and he half expected to glimpse bats flitting above his head. Halting, Sam glanced at the dusty plaques lining one wall. Past sports' winners. Some went all the way back to 1960. He knew if he looked hard enough, he'd probably be able to locate his own name among them. Beside the plaques ran notice boards of current events. By 'current', they had occurred within the last ten years. Swimming and sports carnivals. Cross country events. Along the other wall, tall glass panels made up rows of dirty windows. He frowned in distaste.

Seriously, the cleaner ought to be sacked.

Something made Sam halt again. *What the—?* A loud buzzing noise on the windowpanes made him squint in their direction. That was when he noticed the flies— *hundreds of flies*—small black bodies colliding with the glass in their desperate attempt to escape. With an involuntary gasp of horror, Sam stepped back. He couldn't believe what he was seeing. The bottom of the pane was piled with shrivelled black bodies and disembodied wings. They waited for the cleaner's brush that never came to sweep them all away. Thousands upon thousands.

He was staring at a fly graveyard!

An old, stained fan whirled overhead, its dull *wump wump wump* made Sam look up. He caught a faint whiff of ammonia mingled with the dust in the air. It was exactly how he had remembered this building from long ago. Of course, it was ridiculous to feel this apprehensive that it caused his heart to race in his chest. That was how he felt when he watched horror movies. After all, it was his idea to come, not his wife's frequent promptings.

He shook his head. What *had* he been thinking coming here like this?

With horror and loathing, Sam stared at that closed door at the end of the corridor. *I can't go through with this. They said he was strange—!*

He turned to go when a faint sound paralysed his legs and he couldn't retreat. A sixth sense told him that the door had opened and its enigmatic occupant stood watching him. Sam spun around and swallowed a lump in his throat the size of an egg.

The figure that stood in the shadows was tall and lean. Then the figure stepped into the dim corridor and Sam noticed that he had the palest face he had ever seen. A face that belonged to someone who rarely ventured outdoors into sunlight. It was even whiter than paper. The man wore a crisp, funeral-black coat and long black pants. A turquoise-coloured tie folded immaculately studded his throat. Oiled, jet-black hair looked rubbery as it sat in perfect ripples on his head and pale blue eyes stared at Sam with the sharpness of a physician's scalpel. He glanced over the man's shoulder into his office, a dark cave of ghoulish horrors. He half expected to see a skull lamp sitting on his desk and black candles flickering about the shelves.

Sam cleared his throat. 'Ah ... hello Mr Jones.'

'Mr Rogers?' The man extended his hand. 'I'm so glad you came. Have you thought about my proposition?'

The pulpy-soft hand felt icy. Sam coughed to hide his nervousness. He had to go through with it now, no matter how uneasy he felt.

'Ah ... yes, I'd love to ... ah ... dress up as the Easter Bunny at the Easter school parade.'

The Tree in Piper's Field

Summary: Lil decides to leave her carers' home and seek the one person who might offer her a better life: her uncle Jim. The only thing is, he has amnesia from the accident that tore his family apart and can't remember Lil.

It was almost Christmas when the ancient fig tree in Piper's Field stirred from its long slumber. Of course, the birds that rested in its boughs sensed nothing unusual. An emu paused and blinked up at the tree with its amber eyes. But it looked like any other fig with its mass of spreading foliage and buttressing roots.

In silence, the emu picked a grasshopper off a blade of spiky grass before it strolled away. The fig creaked as it stretched and in the centre of its trunk, a gaping hole yawned. Languid from the heat of the sun, its branches swayed in the rising wind. Leaves and twigs rattled like discordant chimes.

It was about then that the tree sent out the call.

Halfway across the city, Lil Stevens heard a whisper at the edge of her dreams. Upon waking, she quickly dressed and slipped out of her carers' house with the ease of a shadow. The Murrays had been taking care of her since her parents and aunt had died. Lil knew that when they woke up, her absence would be discovered, the police would be called and it would only be a matter of time before they found her.

With her hoodie drawn up over her head, she walked lethargically on the edge of the highway. The air was cool from the night before and although she had hiked far, the morning's brisk wind made her shiver. The two chocolate bars she'd managed to pilfer from the service station ten kilometres back were long consumed and her grumbling stomach felt like an empty chasm. But hunger was not her main concern. Lil knew it was pointless feeling anxious about cars speeding past her; if any slowed down, then she would have to take to the bush and run for her life.

Luckily, the town of Blackheath was up ahead and it had a train station. At least on the train she'd be able to rest her sore feet and fill her water-bottle from a bubbler. She just didn't know what she would do if there was a ticket inspector on board since she had no money left in her purse. Surely out here, commuters weren't checked regularly.

The long walk was refreshing and the peaceful morning drained all the tension from Lil's weary body. She was able to concentrate on what she'd do when she arrived at Piper's Field, her uncle's farm. Memories sifted through her thoughts from the scrappy photo she kept in her pocket. One corner was torn off and it was faded in the middle where she'd folded it. Every so often, she took it out and studied it.

In the middle of a field, there had been a rusty windmill with only five paddles. Beside it stood the most amazing fig tree in the world. During school holidays, her parents had visited the farm and Lil had climbed its sturdy branches and watched the busy cars on the highway whiz by. Overlooking that field on a hill was her uncle's farmhouse. He was her only surviving relative and the photo showed him and her aunt standing side by side, smiling at the camera. Would he be at home for Christmas? Lil didn't believe in or expect miracles, but it made sense that they'd happen at Christmas if they were real.

She checked her watch. 1:30. In the distance, a train was pulling into the station. Throwing back her hood, she quickened her pace.

As Lil was checking her watch, in a crowded shopping centre, Jim Piper finished paying the woman at the fish shop and left with his white parcel of prawns. Late Christmas shoppers were jostling each other and pushing laden trolleys through the maze of people. It was so irritating. He was looking forward to spending a quiet Christmas this year, perhaps watch some carols or an old-fashioned movie on TV.

Since his wife's death last autumn, life had been unpredictably lonely. The amnesia he'd suffered in the car crash still teased him with its missing pieces in his memory. Important details he wished he could remember were like broken mirror fragments that spun in useless circles inside his bruised mind, flashing scenes that made no sense.

Jim tossed the parcel onto the passenger seat of his ute, started the engine and headed down the road. The ute bounced up and down over the deep ruts all the way up the hill, past the windmill and the fig tree. He and his wife had often picnicked under its wide crown and talked about their hopes and the future. Seeing it now weighed him down with bitterness. The sting of sorrow pricked his heart. He brushed away the moisture that unexpectedly blurred his vision.

A sudden image flashed across the screen of his mind and a sharp breath caught in his throat.

The image was of a girl with honey-coloured hair and blue eyes ...

Yes, there had been a girl in the car! He rubbed his forehead with the tips of his fingers and saw her face in his mind again. If only he could remember who she was. He crunched the gears in frustration and sped past.

Jim parked near the house, grabbed his walking stick with one hand and slouched out of the ute holding his prawns with the other. Glancing up, he noticed gathering cumulous clouds like dark cauliflowers filling the sky. The odd spit of rain was already falling. His aching joints told him that lots of rain was on the way. If it was a good fall, maybe he wouldn't have to buy water for his empty tanks this year.

Lil stopped to catch her breath. She growled at the dark sky. Rain was not part of her miracle. When she reached the train platform, she filled her water bottle from the bubblers and then sat on one of the seats away from the other commuters. It was not long before a train pulled in and Lil stepped into the last carriage. Except for a young mother rocking her baby in a pram, it was empty. Lil sighed as her aching body sank into a seat. It felt luxurious, even if it was ripped and sunken in the middle. With no one about, she raised her legs onto the opposite seat and removed spiky goat's head burs from her socks.

Then Lil settled back, placed her head against the seat and felt the rhythm of the train spreading through her tired body. It felt so relaxing. A poem by Robert Louis Stevenson she'd learnt at school crept into her dreamy thoughts: *Faster than fairies, faster than witches, bridges and houses, hedges and ditches ... all of the sights of the hill and the plain fly as thick as driving rain ...*

Her eyes snapped open and she jerked upright. The rocking motion of the train had sent her to sleep! And it *was* raining! Alarmed, she slid to the edge of the seat and gazed out the window at the blurred countryside speeding past. The inclement weather complicated matters for Lil. She had no wet weather clothing to put on and no umbrella.

The train slowed and then stopped to collect more passengers. Lil craned her neck to see who embarked. Heavy rain splattered the windows and the platforms looked slick and slippery. People in raincoats huddled close to the sliding train doors, grasping umbrellas and bags of shopping. Thankfully, no one gave her a second glance.

A few minutes later, the train pulled out and continued on its journey. Lil stood up, pulled her hoodie over her head and walked to the sliding door, clutching the handrail. When the train stopped again, Lil stepped out and, head down against the lashing rain, hurried away from the station. Everything was going so well when a man's voice suddenly called out from behind.

Lil spun around and noticed a policeman hurrying toward her. It was her worst nightmare. She hadn't come this far just to get caught. Without a second thought, she turned and ran down the street. Another shout rose behind her but she didn't look back. Lil didn't know where she was running to or how close the policeman was; she was a rabbit fleeing a hungry fox. She was following an elusive whisper calling in the wind.

Leaving the streets behind, she climbed a fence and shouldered through wet bushes. Stepping into a field, Lil noticed the majestic fig tree with its sweeping branches reaching toward her like warm, beckoning arms. And there was the windmill—*with five paddles!*

As if in a dream, she stumbled towards the tree. Her clothes were wringing wet and her shoes squelched. Her legs wobbled like soft custard beneath her. She stopped to catch her breath beneath the shadowy branches, on bare, dry ground. Through the curtain of rain, she saw her uncle's farmhouse on top of the hill.

Jim grabbed a beer from the fridge, his prawn and thousand-island-dressing sandwich and sat on the porch to watch the rain and ponder the image of the girl he'd seen on the road. With plate on his lap and beer on the floor beside his chair, he began to eat his sandwich, straining to relive that day last autumn. He had taken three mouthfuls when a movement in the field caught his eye.

What the—?

Jim sat up and peered through the driving rain. Someone was out there!

He placed the remainder of his sandwich on the plate and rubbed his sleeve across his eyes. The figure was wearing a hoodie and jeans, so Jim couldn't tell if it was a girl or a boy. *What on earth was he or she doing out in the rain so far from anywhere?*

He pushed himself up off the chair and headed to the ute. He drove across the field, over the furrows, until he was close enough to determine the youngster was a girl. He clambered out and hobbled towards her as she pushed herself onto her feet beneath the fig tree.

'I noticed you out here in this rain,' he said. 'You all right?'

'Jim Piper?' she asked, ignoring his question.

He started and peered at the girl. 'Yes?'

'Please ... look at this,' she said, holding a scrap of paper for him to take. Jim frowned at her. Something familiar—

'Please,' she urged and waved the paper in the air.

Jim's gaze lowered. He drew a sharp breath and took the wet, torn paper she was holding. It showed a photo of him and Sarah, his wife, standing under the fig tree. But how did this girl obtain it? Who was she? He peered into her face, at those teary blue eyes looking back at him. Then the memory of the girl flooded back.

There had been a storm and lots of rain that day, too. He saw Sarah lying in their mangled car after they had crashed down an embankment, his own body pinned and unable to reach her. A child—*a girl*—had been in that car but was thrown clear. After that, his world descended into murky darkness, lots of hospital visits, confusion and loss.

He gasped.

'Lilette?' he muttered.

She nodded. Tears streaked down her cheeks.

'I remember now,' he said. 'We were caring for you after your parents died.'

That's right, she wanted to add, but she was all choked up. *But then you also had a car crash. Aunt Sarah died and you went to hospital for a long time.* 'They put me with carers who told me you'd died.'

'Well, they were wrong,' Jim said, his own eyes filling with warm tears. 'Let's get out of this rain. Then we'd better go and sort out this mess.'

As they climbed into the ute and drove away, the rain stopped and the sun shone over Piper's Field once more. Fond memories drifted through the fig's branches and its leaves quivered with contentment as it sensed a bright future for the two in the farmhouse on top of the hill.

Bully

Summary: _It's difficult to avoid the school bully, especially when you know you've done something to deserve him bashing you up. That's what happens to Reece one day._

"Psst! Reece!"

A slip of paper was shoved into my hand. We were in the middle of a maths lesson, so I had to wait until Mrs Thorne's back was turned to the class before I could peek at it.

Bonecrusher wants to talk to you.

I could feel the blood drain from my face as I looked at my friend and mouthed, _Why me?_

He shrugged and shook his head. The rest of the morning was a blur and all I could think about was meeting Horace Boneto, or Bonecrusher, as he was nicknamed. He was the meanest bully in the school and no one in their right mind messed with him.

What does he want with me? What did I do?

I tried to think, but my mind was fuzzy with everything that had happened that morning. The day had started out just like any other. Except, of course, there was that incident with the bags outside the classroom when everyone took off for recess.

I had opened my chocolate milk all over someone's bag, but it had been an accident. Now that I come to think about it, that bag had looked a bit like Bonecrusher's with all those crazy psychedelic skulls on it. Naturally, I was nice and tried to clean the milk off, but my foot became caught in one of the bag straps that snapped apart when I pulled it free. That was an accident, too.

I was so upset that I lost my balance and stepped on someone's history project sitting behind me on the floor beside his bag. It was a ship made out of paddle-pop sticks, but I swear I didn't see it! I did try to reglue the mast. How could I know the deck was so flimsy that the whole ship would fall apart if I picked it up?

The bell rang and halfway to the canteen, someone called my name. At first, I pretended not to hear them and kept on walking faster and faster, hoping it was just my imagination. I could see the line up ahead; it wasn't too long and there was a teacher standing there. Good! If I could just make it—

A hand grabbed the back of my jumper and I swung around. *Oh no!* My worst nightmare was staring me in the face. Bonecrusher was standing there with his hands on his hips, along with *all* his gang. My heart almost leapt up my throat and out my chest; it was pounding like a machine gun at rapid fire. A cold hand seemed to have knotted my stomach into a tight ball and was squeezing all the bile out.

For a dreadful moment, I thought that everything I had eaten that day would come gushing up from my stomach and explode out of my mouth. That wouldn't be so good either, especially with Bonecrusher standing right in front of me. He would take the full impact.

The look on his face could have cracked the canteen's brick wall. I swallowed the lump in my throat and tried to catch the teacher's attention, but her back was to me.

Rats!

"Heard you were in the State soccer team," Bonecrusher said, his beady eyes boring into mine like an auger.

My gaze drifted towards the teacher again. I couldn't help it. If I was going to be hammered into the ground, I'd make sure she'd hear my pitiful cries for help.

"I'm gettin' some guys together for the comp," Bonecrusher was saying ...

Did it hurt, having a broken nose and a black eye? I opened my mouth to scream—

What? What did he just say?

A crooked smile cracked Bonecrusher's face in two. I could see all of his six yellow teeth gleaming at me in the sunlight.

"So, you wanna be in our team? We need someone with your talent to beat the opposition. What do you say?"

The Dare

Summary: Sometimes bullying can take on a brand-new level of fear. When Scott, Simon's older brother, gave him a terrifying dare to complete, he's somewhat mystified and a whole lot pleased when it comes back to haunt his brother.

BOOM! Scree! Scree! BOOM!

Thunder rumbled overhead and streaks of lightning split the night sky in two. Simon clutched his blankets with tight fists and drew them up over his head. He hated the sound the eucalypt branches made in the wind as they scraped against his bedroom window. His mother often said he imagined things, peculiar things. His teacher once wrote on his report card that he had a vivid imagination, but he didn't think it was written in a positive way because she still gave him a D for story writing.

But sometimes *things* were real, like the skeleton trying to claw its way into his room tonight. Those weren't branches scratching at the glass but its long, bony fingers. He could see them during bright flashes of lightning. Huddled beneath the blankets, he listened to the thunder and that skeleton scratching outside, wanting to come in and strangle him. Only when he thought he might suffocate did he slowly peal back the blankets so he could take a deep breath and glance around his dark room. With every fibre of his being, he tried to stop thinking scary thoughts. Through sheer exhaustion he drifted off to sleep, tossed on a sea of troubled dreams where he was chased across a moonlit field by dozens of frenzied skeletons.

When Simon awoke in the morning, he was lying on his side facing the window. A thin branch swayed in the breeze. The sun was bright and warm as it streamed into his bedroom, forming golden puddles on his rug. The skeletons were gone.

He walked to the window and gazed across the cornfield. At the corner of the rows of corn stood an old scarecrow with its arms stretched out either side of its straw body. It looked crucified, like Christ, with its unseen head lolling forward beneath a black, wide-brimmed hat scored with holes. On its straw body hung a black, tattered coat with a single, silver button, and faded black trousers sat twisted on its straight, pole-stiff legs.

Simon blinked. *That's strange. It's never faced the house before.* And he'd never noticed the shiny silver button on its coat before either. Maybe last night's wind moved it out of its usual place. Simon slipped into his school uniform and raced downstairs with his schoolbag banging against his left shoulder. Scott, his older brother, was already sitting at the kitchen table eating toast. Mum was popping more bread into the toaster. Dad wandered in with a cup of coffee and sat down. He smiled at Simon.

'Storm keep you awake last night?' he asked.

Scott snickered as he buttered his toast. Simon frowned. 'Not really. Slept like a baby.'

Scott laughed. 'That's because you *are* a baby!'

'I am not!' snapped Simon, balling his right hand into a fist under the table.

'That'll do boys!' Mum called from the kitchen.

Simon hated his brother's teasing and tense silence reined while they ate. Oblivious, Dad read the paper and drank his coffee.

'Dad, did you move the scarecrow yesterday?' Simon asked.

Dad folded the paper and looked at him. 'No, why? Is it still there? The wind hasn't knocked it over, has it?'

'No, it's still there,' Simon said. 'It's just that it's facing the house now.'

Scott laughed. 'That's because it wants to get you Simon! *Woooo!*'

He used a spooky voice and wiggled his fingers in front of Simon's face. Peeved, Simon pushed his brother's hands away and glared at him.

Dad placed the paper down and looked at Scott. 'You heard your mother. That'll do.'

Simon knew if he just ignored him, Scott wouldn't tease him as much. But no matter what he said or did, his older brother always managed to push his buttons. If only he wasn't so small for a twelve-year-old. Four years older, Scott was already as tall as their father, well-built and good looking. Several girls at his school even had their eyes on him.

Miserably, Simon bit into his toast and looked out the window. He glimpsed the scarecrow's hat above the waving corn. *I shouldn't have mentioned it.*

Upstairs, Scott cornered him. 'Hey Simon, are you scared of that old scarecrow?'

Simon frowned. 'Why should I be?'

'Because old Jimmy told me it was cursed.'

'He did not! You're a liar!' Simon glared at him. He tried to hold his emotions in check. They were boiling over. 'The scarecrow's harmless and you know it!'

When did Scott ever talk to old Jimmy, anyway? He was an Aboriginal worker Simon's family had inherited along with the farm years ago. Simon had seen him wandering through the cornfields or washing at the water tank behind the house, but he had never spoken to him. Jimmy's skin was dark as coal but his hair was long, white and wispy like summer clouds. His dark eyes looked straight into your soul. Simon's Dad had been too soft to fire him and now he was part of the place, allowed to sleep in a meagre room in the barn and given a small wage, which Dad handed him each Friday in an envelope.

Scott shrugged. 'Suit yourself. But don't say I didn't warn you.' He then shoved Simon up against the wall. 'Tell you what, if you think you're so brave, I dare you to go and take its button after school.'

Simon tried to swallow the gravel in his throat. Scott smiled fiendishly. 'If you don't, I'll spread the word that you still wet your bed at night.'

'That's a lie!'

'Yeah, but they won't know that.' Scott sneered. 'So, how about it?'

Simon hung his head. He felt trapped. The kids at his school were cruel and could taunt forever. 'All right, I'll do it! Let go!'

'That's a good boy,' Scott said, released him and gave Simon's head a rough smack.

All day at school, Simon's thoughts were on the scarecrow. He imagined it lifting its head. Did it have a straw face under that black hat? Or a wizened pumpkin one with eyes, nose and a mouth carved long ago into its faded orange skin? Or was there a skeleton beneath that coat, a real person who had been killed and placed on a stake to resemble a scarecrow? He didn't want to think about it and tried to concentrate on his maths.

Eating his lunch was impossible with skeletons scratching inside his skull. He sat on the sideline of the boys' footy game and told them he didn't feel so well when they asked him to join in. It was a lie, but hey, it was kind of true. His teacher remarked on how pale he looked after lunch and agreed he was unwell. He lay on the stretcher bed in sickbay. But that was worse as he had the whole afternoon to imagine terrible things. In the end, he dragged his feet back to class, his mind overwhelmed by trepidation.

On the bus ride home, Simon thought he was going to throw up. It was only a short ride and then he would have to prove himself to Scott and fulfil the dare. He tried to think of ways he could get out of it. Maybe if he told his parents he hadn't been well at school Scott might show compassion and let him off. Or maybe he could sneak into their house unnoticed, the back way, and talk to mum in the kitchen until dinner time. Or maybe Scott had forgotten all about the dare; Simon knew he hadn't. His brother was indiscriminately nasty and would carry out his threat if he didn't get that silver button.

At last, the bus slowed down and idled near their gate while he got off. He noticed Scott waiting for him near their mailbox, schoolbag on his shoulder and huge grin on his tanned face. Simon's heart sank into his school shoe. He gave a ragged sigh, picked up his schoolbag and dragged his feet off the bus.

'Hey bro. Ready for your dare?' Scott hooked a painful arm around Simon's shoulders. 'The scarecrow's closer from here than from the house.'

Simon felt sick. He nodded. 'Yeah.'

'Come on then.'

Scott dragged his brother along with his strong arm about Simon's neck. Simon shuffled along like a captive. He didn't want to face the scarecrow at all! He wanted to lash out with his fist and scream and kick at Scott. But he was too frozen with fear to do anything.

Finally, Scott halted and removed his arm. He clamped his hands on Simon's shoulders and looked into his frightened eyes.

'Now, I know you are brave and would like to do this on your own,' Scott said with a smug grin, 'so I'll leave you here. Remember, all you need is his button and I'll be satisfied. To make it easy on you, I'll carry your bag home. Got some scissors?' He waited as Simon fossicked for a few moments inside his pencil case for his scissors. Scott smiled. 'There, now you're all set. See ya later bro.'

Simon watched his brother stroll down the dirt road to their house carrying both school bags. The sun was low and afternoon shadows from the surrounding eucalypt forest were beginning to creep across the top of the field. Among the cornstalks he thought he saw a dark face. He stood frozen, wondering if it was just a shadow. Except for the wind rustling through the corn, there was silence.

He took a deep breath to steady his nerves.

It was a short walk through the corn aisles to where the scarecrow stood, though Simon had never been there before. His feet moved by themselves. Soon he came to the corner where the scarecrow stood. Simon stopped. His mouth was dry and his heart was thumping a rapid beat.

For a long time, he stared at the scarecrow, at the black hat perched on top of its downcast head, at the shabby black coat with the shiny silver button. The rest of the effigy was just very old straw stuffed into the long sleeves of the coat and faded legs of the black trousers. On its feet were old black boots encrusted with age-old mud. Lifting it above the waving stalks of corn was a pole up its back.

Simon stared at the hat, imagining it lifting and a wicked face smiling at him just as he reached for the button. *Stop that!* He told himself. It's just straw. Even so, the fear was real and threatened to send him running. He took another deep breath, stepped up to the scarecrow and cut off the silver button.

Suddenly, a gust of wind blew through the cornfield and the coat, bereft of its only button, swung open to reveal the scarecrow's chest of straw. Terrified, Simon turned and ran without stopping in the direction of his house. A cruel wind nipped at his heels as it hurried after him, flinging dirt through the cornstalks. He didn't stop running until he reached the front door.

He swung it shut behind him and latched it. Panting, he stared through the screen at the rustling stalks of corn in case he was pursued. Then he bounded upstairs to look at the scarecrow from his window, to see if it had followed him. It was still there, its coat flapping in the wind. Simon let out a long breath and sagged against his bed. The button was still in his fist. Relaxing his fingers, he stared at it, at the rough-edged, weather-beaten button. It was nothing special, but he knew he had to give it to his brother. Not wanting to face him, Simon crept into Scott's room, placed the silver button on his desk and hurried out.

That night, another storm swung in from the north. Thunder boomed over the farmhouse and the wind howled like a banshee. The branch outside Simon's window scratched on the glass and again he hid beneath his blankets.

During the night, a blood-curdling scream rang through the farmhouse. Simon's eyes snapped open in alarm. His heart raced as footsteps ran past his bedroom door. He could hear the voices of his parents and Scott's loud cry. *Scott?!* Simon clambered out of bed, opened his door and blinked at the lights switched on in the hall. Scott was crying hysterically and Mum and Dad were trying to calm him down.

'I tell you a horrible voice came from outside my window!' Scott screamed. 'Someone was calling, *"give it back! Give it back!"* over and over.'

'There's no one there, son,' Dad said.

Simon hurried back to his room and peered out the window, through the curtain of steady rain at the scarecrow. A shadowed figure with long, wispy white hair was moving back into the cornfield away from their house. A broad smile spread across Simon's face and he clambered back into bed.

The Landing

Summary: *Somewhere in Africa, an airship crash-lands. But the occupant is anything but human. Found by natives and a missionary, Quill is led to their village where she believes she's about to meet another Trillionite from her planet. But what happens when the newcomer is her worst enemy?*

My eyes flicker open. Pain ignites across my left shoulder like fire. I don't even know how it got jammed between the wall and console. Carefully, I ease myself out of the cramped position and mentally assess if anything is broken. Nothing. I've survived the crash.

Red, green and yellow lights flash at me. I blink, trying to focus on the screen that fades in and out. The pod is failing. Not surprising after the incredible heat from the atmosphere and the hard impact. But where have I crashed? What planet?

All the information I need is right before me on that screen. It's faint now. It shows this planet is a closed system and can produce everything its inhabitants need for survival. It has a very similar atmosphere and tree content to that of my home, so even if my pod is irreparably damaged, it won't matter. That's comforting to a newcomer like me. I just hope the others made it …

With my right hand, I unstrap myself, open the hatch above my head and push it back. Overhead is a pretty blue firmament. A sky, not unlike my own. I'm hesitant to breathe in the atmosphere, but there seems to be enough carbon dioxide in it.

Something swift shoots across my vision and involuntarily, I sit up to take a better look. It had two appendages on its sides to help it fly. Wings?!

I'm in a small clearing and all around me is a green forest. A cacophony of strange sounds echo from its heart. It's eerie hearing the alien lifeforms so close to living trees that don't want to harm them.

I ease myself out of the pod and place my feet on the ground. It's soft and cushiony beneath my fibrous boots. I don't possess any weapons and I feel vulnerable out here in the open. After a hasty glance around me, I close the hatch and hurry toward the shelter of the trees.

My name is Quill and I'm not human. I'm a Trillionite. My planet was invaded by Bugadonians and I was one of the fortunate ones to escape. It was beautiful, with a perpetual summer which the Elders originally believed gave rise to the trees' natural intelligence and malice toward each other before the first wave of wars began.

That's also when my people's metabolism began to change. Perhaps it was a form of natural selection that coincided with the intellectual growth of the trees. Some suspected secret Bugadonian technology that somehow stimulated the trees to rouse from their slumber and kill each other. But no one really knew. Now it doesn't matter. My planet is gone.

When the second year of tree wars began, the Bugadonians came in their thousands and started to systematically wipe out all other life-forms on our planet, including us. In haste, our scientists managed to create twenty silver, streamlined pods that resembled seeds. Twenty of the youngest and strongest were sent into space, with the hope that a fragment of these might survive to keep our race from extinction.

My pod crash-landed here. This is my story.

Alien trees surround me. I breathe in their fragrance, the spices, the earthiness, and I feel at home. Branches entwine about each other. I sense no animosity among them, only a mutual closeness. And of course, they are all asleep and unaware of me as I pass beneath their dark canopy, brushing my fingers against their rough bark. Insects sing a choir of constant music. The air is humid and the leaves drip with moisture. It's peaceful and serene. The inhabitants of this planet are fortunate the trees live in harmony with them. But I sense it's just a matter of time before things change. Before the Bugadonians find this planet too.

A sudden movement catches my eye.

Near the mossy trunks, six bipedal aliens observe me. They are brown-skinned, like the trees. Their noses are pierced with long bits of what looks like white bone. Are they men? No one moves.

I'm aware of the increase in my heartbeat. What shall I do? I don't feel ready to confront any life-forms yet. I feel afraid and alone. Every decision I make from now on will mean life or death.

One of them lifts a brown arm with a long thin tube, which the alien places in his mouth. He points it at me. I know I should meld, but I'm fascinated by what he's doing.

I gasp at a stinging pain in my neck that sends me stumbling back. I've been hit by something. I reach up and pull a dart out of my neck, its tip coated purple. *Poison?!* It's all over my fingers. I wipe it on the tree beside me. I'm so stupid for trusting them not to harm me.

My vision blurs and the aliens hurry toward me. I have to get away. My legs feel heavy and it's difficult to think and move. I have to make an attempt to meld.

With my remaining strength, I shove my hand inside the nearest tree, but before I complete the transition, I collapse against the bark and darkness obscures my eyes.

'Wake up!'

I start as someone shakes my shoulder. My eyes snap open. The brown-skinned aliens stand around me, staring, but they look frightened, too. That's because one of my arms and most of one side of my body has melded with the tree. The one shaking me has tanned skin and blue eyes. And he has more clothes on his body than the others.

'What happened here?' he asks, genuinely amazed, gesturing to the tree where I'm slumped with half my body inside it.

I can understand what you're saying.

'Are you all right?' he asks. 'What happened to your body?'

'I'm all right,' I reply and extract myself from the tree to loud gasps and frightened whispers.

The man stumbles back from me and his eyes grow enormous. He stares at the side of my body that melded, clearly shocked by what I just did. I don't move.

'*What* are you?' he asks.

I can't afford to tell him. My body aches from the substance in the dart and I feel too dizzy to attempt an escape. Besides, there are too many of them. If I melded into the tree now, they might burn it down or poison it on my account. I would be trapped inside.

The man steps forward again and offers me his hand. 'You're too weak to remain here. Come.'

The brown-skins move back as he helps me to my feet. I sway but the man's hand steadies me. His touch is sweaty and hot. He must be warm-blooded. Our blood is cold and we need the sun like the trees to survive.

One part of me is terrified at the thought of going with these aliens; another part is curious and reckless. That part of me yearns to learn more about this world and it prevails.

The man holds my hand, not tightly, as he leads me through the jungle. Sometimes he speaks and I like that.

'My name is Olaf,' he says. 'I'm a missionary here with the Mogaby tribe. You scared them witless with what you did back there. They think you're a demon. Guess you'll talk more later on, when you've had a rest. Are you thirsty?'

He hands me a worn, leather-bound bottle on a long strap with liquid inside. Once he unscrews the lid, I smell it but the liquid has no scent.

'It's all right,' he says. 'It's just tepid water. Sorry it's not cold, but ice is a luxury we don't have here.'

I prefer tepid water so I drink and drink until he removes it from my thirsty mouth. 'That's enough. You'll make yourself sick if you drink anymore.'

I watch as he screws on the cap and places the bottle over his shoulder. Then he looks me up and down curiously.

'Where are you from?' he asks again and, not really meaning to, I glance up at the sky. The expression on his face shows he understands my cryptic gaze. 'An alien, eh? Well, I can't imagine why you'd be out here. I've only seen the natives in seven long years, so you might enlighten me with news from the stars.'

I don't think he believes me by the way he chuckles. He turns and we trudge through the balmy jungle. I notice sweat pooling on the back of his khaki shirt and under his arms. Its pungent. Being cold-blooded, we Trillionites never sweat. We thrive in hot, humid temperatures.

After about an hour of slow walking, Olaf stops and looks at me. 'There's something I want to show you back at the village.'

My curiosity piques. What could he possibly want to show me? Then, through the trees, I notice wooden buildings and more brown-skins walking about with young ones. There are also four-legged creatures that wander up and sniff my legs. I jerk back from them, afraid, but when

Olaf claps his hands they scurry off with their tails between their back legs. Strange creatures that whimper.

The brown-skins whisper and stare. They all look frightened, but I wouldn't hurt any of them; that's not my mission here.

Olaf leads me to a grass-roofed hut and gestures for me to enter. The brown-skins remain outside, but they don't move away. Inside the hut, there's a rough wooden table, some chairs and a bed standing against a wall with what appears to be a lumpy mattress on top.

'This is where I live,' says Olaf and wipes his brow.

We sit on the chairs and already I feel claustrophobic. We Trillionites yearn the open spaces and trees. Here I feel trapped, smothered by the close air. I wonder when he'll show me what he wanted me to see. He clasps his large hands on the table and looks across at me.

'Who are you?' he asks again.

'My name is Quill,' I tell him.

'That's a start. Now, are you really an alien?'

I nod. He starts and sits back in his chair. 'Are there any more of you here?'

Again, I nod.

'It's just that … I found another one of your people in the jungle last month.'

My heartbeat increases and now it's my turn to be startled. I realise it's a *who* and not a *what* that Olaf wanted to show me. One of my kin. Excitement courses through my body.

'Wait here,' Olaf says, strides through the open door and is gone.

I stand up and move to the doorway. Brown-skins, crouched on haunches, watch me from a distance. I start to pace inside the hut when I hear footsteps outside and hurry to the door. My blood vibrates in my veins, a sign of great joy.

Then I see him, walking beside Olaf. He's so much like me, a Trillionite, except—

His speckled eyes give his species away.

A Bugadonian!

I panic inside and search for a way out. There's none. I cannot allow myself to be captured by my enemy. I dive through the doorway and run as hard and as fast as I can into the jungle. Already, startled brown-skins give chase. I hear their quiet feet behind me, but I am swifter and I won't be captured again. Not when the Bugadonians have landed here too.

With haste, I push my hands and arms inside a huge tree, then the rest of my body also until there's no sign of me. It's warm and safe within. The tree shuts out the world with all its dangers. I know Olaf, the brown-skins and the Bugadonian will search for me, each for different reasons, but I'll remain hidden until darkness falls. Then I'll move on and search for the rest of my people. I'll shut my eyes and sleep till then.

Max's New Book

Summary: _Max Mouse is writing his latest book, but it's not a How To this time. He's had lots of rejections so far, so will this latest book get published? Read on and find out._

'Oh my whiskers and tail!' exclaimed Martha Mouse. 'Where's Max?'

'He's writing another book, Mama,' said Mindy with a little giggle.

'What? Not another one! After ten rejections, I thought he'd learnt his lesson!'

Martha clutched the rejection letter in her apron pocket, the latest one from Grey Whiskers Publishing Hole to Max. It had not only made him sad, but her as well. She remembered reading it over Max's shoulder when he opened it and tears filled her eyes.

Dear Max Mouse,

We cannot publish your book, How to Ski Down the Farmer's Tractor Wheel, as this is far too dangerous to place in the paws of small pinkies. I'm surprised you even sent it in to us to consider. It's almost as ridiculous as the last one we received from you, How to Give Rides on Your Back to Fairies, especially when there are no such things as fairies in the first *place. (Every pinky knows that!) And wasn't there the book before that titled How to Make Friends with Bulls. Totally out of the question! And then there was Things a Mouse Can do With His Tail. Tickling a cat's nose made one of my editors faint with fright. He hasn't been quite himself since reading your book and is even frightened of his own shadow.*

Max Mouse, the problem with your ideas is that they are too extreme even for grown-up mice, let alone pinkies, to attempt. Please don't send me anymore of your How To books. Stick to reading instead.

Yours sincerely,

Sally Squeaker

(Publisher)

Even now, Martha's heart ached as she remembered how Max's delicate whiskers had wilted and his tail flopped after he had read it. Such hurt on her little pinky's face!

'He said he won't leave his quill until he's finished,' said Malcolm all of a sudden, nibbling on the grain on his plate.

Maybelle grinned. 'But don't worry, mamma, he's almost finished. And it's not a *How To* book this time. It's an adventure story about a scary cat called Puss Without Boots.'

Major Mouse roused from his sleep on the floor in the corner, leapt up and waved his toothpick sword about.

'What ho! Did someone say hairy cats in boots? I'll show them a thing or two—'

Martha hurried to his side and patted his arm. 'It's all right Dad! There's no cats about! Go back to sleep!'

After some ado, Major Mouse complied, shoved his toothpick into his string belt and curled up on the straw again. Pretty soon, he was snoring softly. Martha sighed and turned back to her eight pinkies nibbling on fresh grain.

'Well, if he's almost finished...'

Meanwhile, Max stuck his quill behind his left ear and read the revised story after scribbling out Puss Without Boots. It went like this:

Mouse in Boots

Once upon a time there was a miller who had three sons. When he died, he left his mill to his oldest son who turned it into a home for retired pirates. He left all his alpacas to his second oldest son who went into business with his older brother selling woollen shirts, pantaloons, eye patches and tricorn hats to passing pirates. And last of all, he left a good-looking mouse to his youngest son called Bert because he knew he loved animals. His father also left him his sewing kit.

'Aw, please share the mill with me,' pleaded Bert, after he received his meagre inheritance.

But his brothers just laughed at him and told him to get lost and join a circus, which was the last thing on Bert's mind. He was more worried about where he was going to live and what he was going to eat.

Now the mouse, who had once been a tightrope walker in a real circus, had a lightbulb moment. 'Hey, I've heard the King is depressed and could do with a performance to cheer him up.'

'How on earth did you hear that? And anyway, when could you talk?' Bert asked in awe.

'I always keep my ears to the ground,' the Mouse replied.

'That's easy for you, being so short.' Bert's shoulders sagged. 'But I can't do any tricks or sing or juggle.'

'Leave that to me,' said the Mouse. 'Just get us to the palace and sew me some boots.'

And so, Bert sewed the Mouse some very fancy boots with sweet little bells on them that tinkled as he walked. When they arrived at the palace, the King's crier was just unrolling his long parchment in order to tell all the citizens what the King's troubles were. For a full hour, Bert and the Mouse listened to all his ailments. There was burnt lasagne, gout in his feet, ingrown toenails, pigeons pooing on his balcony and outdoor furniture, frogs proposing to his daughter the princess, his wife falling into the vat of porridge and spoiling his breakfast, fast-growing nose hairs, flies swimming in his soup and terrible performers who were trying to make him laugh.

Max slouched forward on his stool and sighed, which was when Martha knocked on the door.

'Come in,' he called and Martha did.

She came and sat beside him, sensing that something was wrong. 'How is your book getting along?'

'I'm stuck and don't know what to write next,' Max said.

His mother smiled and gave him a hug. 'Oh, that's called *writer's block.*'

'It feels like writer's brick,' said the dejected pinky.

'Come and have some grain and maybe you'll think of the next scene when your tummy is full.'

That sounded like a good idea, so Max followed his mother into the kitchen, where a small plate of grain sat on the table. His eight brothers and sisters were at the end of their meal and were cleaning their whiskers and paws. The Major was still snoring on his straw bed, clutching his wrinkled walnut helmet in his sleep.

Max sat down and nibbled on the grain. Mandy, his little sister, snuggled up beside him.

'How's your writing going?' she asked.

'It's not going anywhere; I've got writer's block,' he told her.

'Does it hurt being blocked?' she asked in an innocent voice.

Max giggled. 'No, it's just annoying not being able to think of the next scene.'

'Well then, let's go drop flies into Scratch's mouth. I think he's sleeping— '

'Mandy!' Martha shrieked. 'Max! I hope that's not what you get up to while my back is turned?'

'Mamma, your back doesn't have to be turned for Max to do that!' laughed Mario. 'He even rolls peanuts across the kitchen floor when the farmer's wife is cooking.'

'Max!' his mother shrieked.

All the excitement woke Major Mouse, who leapt to his feet once more, grappling with his walnut helmet. It ended up flipping out of his fumbling paws and almost hitting a squealing Martha on the head, missing her by a whisker. Max and the pinkies all laughed. It was just what Max needed. Now he was ready to tackle the last part of his book.

'I think I'm unblocked now,' he announced.

'Back to work then, young pup!' gestured Major Mouse with a wave of his paw. 'No time to lose. Tally ho and all that!'

'Remember the nursery rhymes I taught you, Max,' called Martha. And he did.

Back in his room, Max took the quill from behind his ear and wrote:

'I'm going to see the King!' announced Mouse.

'Why?' asked Bert, who couldn't understand why the King would want to see a mouse wearing fancy boots.

'I'm going to perform for him.'

'Ha! The guards won't let you in.'

'Yes they will.'

'No they won't.'

'Yes they will. Now shut up!'

And the Mouse left Bert and made his way over the drawbridge and into the palace. His boots tinkled as he walked and the guards just thought he was someone important and let him through. On the way, he met a talking frog holding a bouquet of flowers in its webbed hands, which he thought was odd since frogs normally couldn't talk. It was on its way to see the princess.

'Hey frog!' called Mouse. The frog stopped hopping and looked at him. 'Do you know there are a lot of good-looking frog-ettes in the moat?'

'How do you know that?' asked Frog, pretending not to be interested.

'I heard them croaking—I mean singing—just then,' lied Mouse. 'See for yourself.'

'My heart already belongs to the princess,' said Frog.

Mouse shrugged. 'Hey, I'm just telling you what I saw and heard. It's up to you who you marry. But I think a frog would be better suited to a frog-ette.'

'That's your opinion!' said Frog and hopped on.

Glancing over his shoulder, Mouse saw the frog stop and stare down at the moat longingly. He also noticed some sheep juggling balls and clubs, but thought no more about it and continued towards the King's court.

Ah, it won't be long before—

A loud splash interrupted Mouse's thought and he turned to look. The bouquet of flowers lay on the ground, but Frog was nowhere to be seen. This made Mouse giggle, upsetting a troupe of blackened-looking fire eaters coming his way.

'Have you just performed before the King?' he asked.

'How can you tell?' one grumbled with smoke trailing from his mouth.

'Well, it's either that or you've burnt his lasagne.'

'The King's not in a good mood,' said another with smoke pouring from both his ears. 'He laughed when one of our troupe burnt himself to a crisp and then kicked us out.'

Max paused, feeling a little blocked again, and pondered what he should write next. He remembered his mother's words about nursery rhymes and something popped into his head. It sounded quite loud. *That must be how writer's un-block*, he thought and licked the end of his quill. His idea went like this:

Just then, a beautiful young girl with raven-black hair came towards Mouse. Oo la la, Mouse thought. Bert might find her attractive and marry her. He could do with a wife instead of a mouse for a companion. As she came closer, Mouse noticed she was crying. Maybe she, too, was a hopeless performer.

'Er, excuse me,' he said.

'Why? What did you do?' asked the girl.

'I didn't do anything. It's just a saying. Have you just performed before the King?'

'No, I've lost my sheep and don't know where to find them. They're all I have in the world. Boo hoo!'

She made such a racket wailing that some guards came along and escorted them from the palace, locking the doors behind them.

'Well, that's that then. What's your name?' Mouse asked the distraught girl.

'Bo-Peep and I've lost some very important sheep.'

'Why are they so important anyway?'

'You don't understand,' Bo-Peep said. 'My sheep were going to perform before the King.'

Mouse snickered. 'Sheep can't do much.'

'They can climb on each other's backs and juggle balls and clubs.'

Mouse nodded. 'That's pretty impressive. Where did you lose your sheep anyway?'

'If I knew that, I'd know where to go look for them!' she said and wailed some more.

Mouse thought his ears would crack or burst or block up from all her crying when he had another idea.

'Come and meet my friend,' he said and introduced her to Bert, who thought she was the prettiest girl in all the land.

They were married right there beside the moat and Frog and a choir of frog-ettes sang at their wedding. Bo-Peep's sheep returned, waggling their tails behind them, and for entertainment, they juggled balls and clubs.

Mouse never did perform before the King, but was given a bag of gold coins because Frog finally left his daughter alone. Mouse had no need for gold coins so he gave them to Bert, who bought himself a cottage in the country, where he and Bo-Peep lived and had twenty children.

The End.

Max placed his quill down and smiled. Then he slipped his manuscript into an envelope, addressed it to Grey Whiskers Publishing Hole and raced to the post office where he bought a stamp.

Exactly one week later, a letter came addressed to Max Mouse. Martha stood behind him with a paw on his shoulder. His brothers and sisters gathered around him too, and he read it out aloud. It said this:

Dear Max Mouse,

We're very pleased to accept your book for publishing. Yes, you've finally made a hit with the mice editors here at Grey Whiskers. They all want to hear more about Mouse's adventures. Perhaps you could write some new stories about him in the future. I'll let you know of its official launch date and you can invite your family and friends.

Yours sincerely,

Sally Squeaker (Publisher)

Martha beamed, proud as punch at her little pinky, and her smile lasted all day long, even when Max chased the fairies around in the garden. He invited them all to his book launch and they threw a party for him. Everyone asked him to read his story to them and he sat on a toadstool in the garden and did just that. He was the happiest little mouse on the farm.

Mouse's Christmas

Summary: *What gift does a little mouse give Henny and Redman Rooster on the event of their eggs hatching at Christmas? Max Mouse sneaks into the farmhouse itself to look for the very best gift of all. Find out what it is by reading the story.*

On Sunday morning, Martha Mouse called her large family into their spacious kitchen under a bright sprig of Christmas bush. Bits of sparkly blue and red tinsel and a shiny gold bauble, cracked on one side, hung above their table. Little Monte had rescued them from the farmer's trashcan before the dumpster arrived on Friday morning. Standing tall and straight next to Martha was Major Mouse, her father, wearing a walnut helmet and toothpick sword stuck in his string belt. Martha twitched her long whiskers as she studied the little mice clustered around her.

'As you all know,' she squeaked, 'next Wednesday is Christmas so I want you all to be on your very best behaviour.'

'We always are, mamma,' giggled little Mandy. She had pretty brown eyes and neat little paws.

Martha straightened Mandy's bow and stroked her ear. 'Well dear, most of you are very good.' She glanced at all the pink ears facing her and the brown gleaming eyes of her pinkies. One was missing. 'Oh my, where's Max? He's always elsewhere!'

'Last time I saw him he was off with the fairies,' squeaked Marcus.

Martha's nose twitched. 'How many times do I have to tell him to leave the fairies alone? He plays so roughly he's likely to pull off one of their wings.'

'No mamma,' whispered Mindy. 'They like to ride on his back through the garden.'

'What ho,' the Major rasped. 'I'll bring the little pup back, don't you worry.'

Martha licked Mabelle's face clean and tweaked Mario's whiskers so they looked straight on his snout. 'Now remember, don't go near Scratch. He may look like he's sleeping, but one of his eyes is always open and watching for a mouse to eat. Go and play in the straw, but don't venture far from our hole.'

'Yes mamma!' twelve pinkies piped up in unison.

Outside in the garden, something bright and fast headed straight for the Major's helmet. The old mouse ducked just in time as a giggling fairy dive bombed him. He waved his toothpick sword at it but missed, scowling. There was a rustling sound in the bushes and then out ran Max Mouse through a grass tunnel with a tiny, laughing fairy sitting on his back grasping his fur. The Major grabbed Max and the fairy flew off with an indignant yell shaking his fist.

'Home with you, young pup,' the Major wheezed.

The Major hauled Max into the kitchen by the scruff of his neck. The little mouse squealed, his tiny legs ran so fast in the air they were a blur when Martha saw him. The Major dropped him in front of his daughter who frowned at the breathless pinky and placed her paws on her hips.

'Max!' she squeaked in a very high voice. 'When will you ever learn not to tease the garden fairies?'

'But mamma,' Max moaned. 'I wasn't teasing them. We were just playing chasings in the long grass.'

Martha squeaked. 'What if you had pulled off one of their delicate wings? We'll have to pay for the damages and we're as poor as church mice. I don't want you to play roughly with them again! Remember it's Christmas next week. Santa Mouse won't leave you anything if you're naughty.'

Max hung his little head. 'Yes mamma.'

'Now go and play with your brothers and sisters.'

His little claws scraped on the stone floor of the kitchen as Max made his way outside. Martha looked at the Major and shook her head.

'There's always one in every litter, isn't there?' she sighed.

The Major pulled out his toothpick sword and waved it about. He stepped back and forth crying 'tally ho' and stabbed at the air. Martha placed her paw on his arm.

'Now don't you start.'

On Monday morning, Maddie and Mindy raced through the hole and into the kitchen. Their long whiskers were waving up and down excitedly and their beady little eyes looked huge. They didn't know whether to giggle or be serious. Martha stopped counting out the grain for lunch and looked at them curiously.

'Mamma,' they squeaked. 'Max is puddle boating in the rain!'

Martha's paws shot to her snout as she gasped. 'Oh my tail and ears! Major, please go see what's happening at once.'

The Major scowled, being woken from his midday nap. He adjusted his toothpick sword and lopsided helmet and dashed outside the hole flanked by Maddie and Mindy. The garden was dripping with fresh rain and whenever the Major ducked under the delicate fern fronds, they showered him with water, making him scowl even more. Maddie and Mindy just giggled behind him.

Ahead, they heard loud, squeaky laughter. Pushing through the long, wet grass, they came to a lake of puddle water where Max was sailing on a ragged slither of bark. Tied to a stick was a dirty rag he'd stuck in the middle and used it for a sail. Wrapped around the top of the stick was a piece of gold tinsel he'd scrapped from somewhere for decoration. Up and down the puddle lake sailed the tiny mouse, the wind blowing his whiskers back. A delirious smile was curled on his little snout and every so often he laughed out loud with glee.

'Oh there's the naughty little pup!' the Major exclaimed and in the next breath called out. 'Max! Come here at once!'

And so, Max was hauled before his mother once again in a filthy state. His fur, wet and muddied, stuck up all over his tiny body and his whiskers were more crooked than Scratch's hind leg. His beady eyes gleamed mischievously. Some of his brothers and sisters raced inside, squeaking, to see what would happen next.

Martha threw her paws into the air and shook her head. 'Just look at the state of your fur and whiskers, Max! What were you thinking? You could have drowned in that puddle! We mice are not good swimmers you know. Major will tell you the tale of poor Uncle Mannie Mouse.'

Major Mouse cleared his throat and placed his paw on Max's head. 'Why, yes, your Uncle Mannie loved to play in the puddles just like you do. But one day, the rain was heavier and the puddles much deeper. He didn't know this of course and fell off his bark boat and simply drowned.'

'So, Max, find something safe to do,' Martha scolded, licking her paws and cleaning the mud off his fur.

'Yes, mamma,' squeaked the tiny mouse, hanging his head.

On Christmas Eve, there was a great commotion in the barn. Redman Rooster was flapping about, telling all the animals that Henny's eggs were finally hatching. They all congratulated him in their special ways. The cow mooed, the sheep bleated and the pig oinked in her pen. They promised to do something special for Henny and Red. When Martha called her pinkies to tell them Henny's good news, Max was absent—*again!*

'Has anyone seen Max?' she squeaked in an anxious voice, looking at her children.

'He told me he was going into the farmhouse to get some bread,' Morris piped up, his jaws full of seed.

'Oh my!' yelped Martha.

The Major jumped up at once, toothpick sword waving in the air and made a valiant dash through the hole toward the farmhouse. Following closely behind was

Martha and all her pinkies. The Mouse family didn't have to go far when there was Max proudly clutching a lump of fresh bread in his paws. Martha ran up and held him by his ears. The Major waved his toothpick sword around, just in case Scratch was about. The pinkies all gathered.

'What were you thinking, Max, going into the very farmhouse?' Martha Mouse waved her paw at him. 'Don't you remember how the farmer's wife cut off the tails of those three blind mice with her carving knife?'

'But I wasn't getting it for myself,' squeaked Max, clutching the piece of bread in his tight paws. 'It's a gift for Henny. She's been sitting on her eggs all day and hasn't eaten anything. I thought she might like fresh bread for Christmas.'

Max's thoughtfulness brought a lump to Martha's throat and she hugged him. 'Well, why don't you go and give it to her? After all, it is Christmas. Look, there she is on her nest.'

The Mouse family followed Max as he carried the bread to Henny's box. The other animals had gathered, too, to look at her brood. From under her wings came the soft chirping sounds of her newly hatched chicks. Redman Rooster was standing nearby, looking proud with his glossy red feathers.

'Thank you all for coming to celebrate with Henny and me,' he clucked.

'We've also brought some gifts,' mooched Jasmine the cow. 'I brought you some nice-smelling new hay for your box, Henny.'

'Thank you Jasmine,' clucked Henny. 'That'll come in handy.'

'And here is some soft wool so your chicks can keep warm at night,' baaed Barbara the old sheep, laying down some of her white wool.

'Oh, thank you Barbara,' clucked Henny. 'The nights have been a bit cold.'

'And I brought you some extra grain to eat,' oinked Peppy the pig.

'Thank you, Peppy,' clucked Henny. 'It'll save me having to go look for it myself.'

Then Martha ushered her pinkies forward. The Major prodded Max out in front, still holding the fresh bread in his tiny paws. At that moment, Martha felt so proud of Max.

'And my littlest pinky, Max, has brought you some fresh bread, straight from the farmer's wife's oven.'

'Ooooh, I love bread!' clucked Henny, her brown eyes gleaming. 'Thank you Max and all the mice.'

Redman strutted forward. 'Max is very brave, the bravest of all the mice.'

'And so say all of us,' agreed the other animals.

Max's ears turned bright pink but he felt very happy all the same. Just then, six little chicks peeped their heads out from under Henny's wings.

'Look!' he squeaked.

And that's just what all the animals did. Henny's face glowed as she clucked. Martha placed her paw on Max's head and wiggled her whiskers.

'Merry Christmas everyone!' she squeaked. She winked at Max, her heart swelling with pride. 'Merry Christmas Max.'